# SPINOSAURUS

## HUGO NAVIKOV

SEVERED PRESS
HOBART TASMANIA

# SPINOSAURUS

WWW.SEVEREDPRESS.COM

ISBN: 978-1-925342-80-2

# PROLOGUE: TSHIKAPA, CONGO

Arthur Mabele dug in the muddy clay of the Vermeulen mines next to the Kasai River, a tributary of the mighty Congo and itself deeper than most rivers in the world. On the other side of the river from the mine is thick rainforest jungle, most of which has never been charted by man, even today. Satellites cannot see through the ceiling of foliage, and there would be little reason to do so anyway—it is a *terra incognita,* which isn't worth the trouble financially, and scientists or others interested in penetrating its mysteries are not the kind who get funding.

But Vermeulen Mining Corp. and other commercial miners of rare earth metals and diamonds *do* find it very financially rewarding to occupy that part of Congo. Diamonds are dug up by hand by the people of the area, some from holes dug fifty feet into the banks of the Kasai where the water has to be pumped out by methods old when the Romans built their aqueducts.

So the miners dig by hand, getting maybe five dollars for a gem that, when cut and polished, will bring ten thousand or more. Diamonds are very plentiful in Tshikapa, so supply and demand keeps prices shrinkingly low and lets Vermeulen and other companies buy them for almost nothing.

Arthur Mabele had been extraordinarily lucky at his mining endeavors, and got his entire family spending fifteen hours a day digging for what passed for treasure there. They lived in the tent city at the mines like everyone else to protect them from the militias that wanted control of Vermeulen's property, but they had a television set and one of those dishes that gets television from space back at home, plus a box that let them watch everything for free.

His favorite show when they took days off, which was infrequently, was *Cryptids Alive!* a show in which the beautiful Ellie White led viewers on a search for mythical creatures that probably actually existed. They had never found one that they could get video of, but that didn't matter. They were always *so* close, and that's what was exciting. It was in English, but that didn't matter—monsters were monsters, and there were lots of "artist's conceptions" and Ellie running toward or away from giant cryptids to keep Arthur and his family mesmerized.

It was night at the mine, too dark to see anything except the security lights on at the Vermeulen building, and Arthur was bone-tired after a day in which he found six rocks—*six*, enough for his family to have something other than gristle and skin for their meal. But, as sometimes happened, his body was too thoroughly worn out for him to immediately fall asleep, so he left his sleeping wife and boy and girl in the tent as he went out to look at the stars. It was relaxing and reminded him that there was a universe outside the diamond mines, a mysterious universe that enchanted him as much as the mysteries on *Cryptids Alive!*

It was also as silent as it got this close to the rainforest's edge. He could hear the cawing birds and the occasional screech of the monkeys, but the sounds themselves were muffled, swallowed by the thick vegetation. That's why he could hear a motorboat revving across the river and landing on the mine's side. That sound was followed by loud whispers and the *slap-slap-slap* of someone in boots running through the mud of the mine area—they had to know what they were doing, because the bank was marked by deep holes and shallow ones—and then between the workers' tents, heading for the far side.

Arthur couldn't make them out well, except as silhouetted by the company building's floodlights, but he could see it was two men in military-type uniforms and caps, one of them carrying ... a big smooth rock? Something inside a sack? Whatever it was, it seemed heavy and the man carrying it let out a huge sigh of relief when he put it down next to the tent closest to the mine complex's entry gate. Then, as far as Arthur could tell since they ran off into the darkness, they left through that way. He heard a vehicle start up and drive off.

Lots of weird things happened in a Congo mine, but this was crazy. The military in Tshikapa never entered the Vermeulen area, it being officially Belgian property, even a poor miner like Arthur Mabele knew that. But the militias who everybody knew wanted control of the mines and to force out the Belgians, they snuck into the mines whenever they could, something butchering the unfortunate workers as a warning not to work for foreigners, to refuse to mine for them so they would leave and the militias could take what "belongs to the people of Congo."

The murders certainly didn't help morale among the miners, but what could they do? They had to work if they were to eat. It wasn't like the militias were inviting them to dinner so they wouldn't have to toil for the Belgians.

Was it a bomb, this thing that the two soldiers had placed next to that far tent? Arthur wasn't religious and had no interest in being a martyr, but he found a mystery even as probably banal as this one irresistible. He stood up from the crouch he had assumed when he heard the men coming and very slowly and silently placed his bare feet in the mud, then the dirt, as he approached the edge of the tent city, where the object lay.

With excitement, he peeked around the corner of the tent— pointlessly, he knew, if it was a bomb; it wasn't like a piece of fabric was going to protect him from an explosion. He didn't have a flashlight and the floodlights from the building illuminated nothing this far away. So he bent down and put his hands on it.

It was smooth, like a river rock. Or an egg. He pushed on it a little and it was so heavy it barely even moved. It had a weird, kind of musty smell, exactly like one would expect from a dredged-up river rock—

*HRANNNNNNNNNNNNNNNNNNNH!*

Arthur almost fell down at the sound, thinking at first a plane from the town's little airport had crashed and blown up. But that wasn't what it sounded like, not really. It was more like a roar. Like a—

*HAAAAARRRRRRRRRRRRRRNNNNNNNNNHHHHH!*

That one was even longer and louder. What in the name of his ancestors *was* that? He couldn't see anything in the dark, but he could see just enough to get back to his family's tent, seeing that many miners had been awakened by the unholy shrieking, snarling, screaming *ROAR* that he could tell had come from the far side of the Kasai.

"Get up! Get up! Come with me!" he roused his family in Swahili, grabbing his children by their arms and dragging them out of the tent until they had woken enough to walk on their own. Arthur's wife was slow to awaken, but once she realized the children were gone, she snapped to and rushed out of the tent to follow her family into the brush on the edge of the tent city.

Some fires had been lit inside tents, no doubt instinctively at the outset of some kind of chaos, and Arthur could see the fires were around rags around tree branches, the fabric doused with cooking oil to make torches.

Another blast from what Arthur knew now had to be some kind of animal, and something raged out of the dense jungle. They could feel more than see the giant *thing's* stomps, which ceased with a splash.

The blood froze in Arthur's veins as he realized what that had to mean: The roaring, epically enraged monster was swimming to the mine side of the river. *Their* side.

Men, being men, had massed with their torches near the water's edge, trying to see what was making the horrifying sounds and making the ground shake beneath their feet. Arthur could see what was going to happen as if it were already a memory, and if he didn't have his wife and little ones with him, he would have shouted to them to get out of the way, *run away, GO!*

But they stayed grouped together, the torches illuminating their patch of ground.

Then the river heaved and the torches showed Arthur the monster climbing out of the water. The light showed a crocodile's head on a lion's body, four legs as thick as an armored car, and, when it crashed down on the screaming men, making the torches fly and set the tents aflame, the huge fin on the *thing's* back. It roared again and now everyone was screaming, some coming out of their tents to run, others huddling and hoping not to be seen.

None of it did any good. Arthur and his family watched in horror as the Kasai Rex—that's what it was, a Kasai Rex, the river monster of legend, a dinosaur that never died out, a predator, a death machine Congolese parents told their children about to scare them into good behavior—stomped and ripped and bit and swallowed and ate, the fire spreading all around it but the building-sized creature not even noticing.

It trampled every tent, killed every single person in the way, until it got to that final tent, the one that the militia had placed the bomb or rock next to, and it let out a roar so loud that it made Arthur's eyes water even though his hands were clamped hard against his ears. Roared and roared and roared until Arthur, his wife, and his children all had been forced into unconsciousness.

***

When Arthur Mabele woke in the light of the morning, his wife was already awake, shaking from cold and fear but watching over their children, who were still sleeping. The tent city was a smoldering mess of mud, bodies, body parts, and ruined wood and fabric.

His wife looked at him and said but one thing:

"Kasai Rex."

Arthur nodded. He had never in his life made an international phone call, never tried to find the number for a telephone in America, but knowing his family was safe, he knew it was his responsibility to tell the world so the Kasai Rex, taller than the Vermeulen building and almost as long as the tent city itself, killer of everything it encountered, could itself be killed.

It took him the better part of a week even to locate a telephone—miners were not welcome inside the Vermeulen building. It took still longer to find where and whom he should contact, and almost three weeks had passed before Arthur could find someone who spoke English *and* Swahili to place the call for him and interpret his story. But finally he was able to tell what had happened, tell the only people he *knew* would believe him.

He called *Cryptids Alive!*

5

# CHAPTER 1

Before I spill my whole story, I need to ask you a question.

Humans: the most dangerous animal. True or false?

They're the most annoying animal, that's for sure. Also the greediest, the best at making weapons and making tools that make weapons, the ones who eat the most food when they're already full, the most superstitious and willing to kill for a little bit of luck or sexual ability, but the most dangerous? No.

Put a Bengal tiger and the world's most vicious human in a room and call me when it's time to mop up what's left of the human. Put Michael Phelps and a hungry Great White shark in thirty feet of water-hell, give Phelps a spear gun and a wetsuit—and see how many more sharks come around once the Olympic hero has been reduced to a froth of blood. Put a twenty-foot chain around the ankle of the most recent Mister Universe and clamp the other end onto the tail of an 18-foot adult King Cobra. In minutes, it'll be time for the Mister Universe runner-up to start fulfilling some duties.

*En masse*, of course, humans are a different story. We can communicate better than any other animal, organize better, procreate better, build and wield weapons unique to anything else on Earth. We also build rules and laws, concepts of justice, ideas that must be dodged and thwarted if individual humans are to fulfill the role of "most dangerous animal."

That is my role. I am a dodger and a thwarter of treaties, handshake agreements, hunting quotas, and any other form of cooperation different states employ to keep men like me from hunting in their forests, their savannahs, their jungles and rivers. I'm proud to say that I have never personally killed any endangered or protected animal by my own hand; there are plenty of men slavering at the opportunity to do that. All I do is lead the humans to the black rhinoceros, whose horn is sheared off the corpse to make into aphrodisiac powder for the Chinese. I help them get close enough to kill elephants with precious ivory in their tusks, the shooters responding to worldwide demand. Same with those seeking silverback gorillas to kill and sell as trophies to the highest bidder.

I suppose, given our zeal for killing despite the laws of nations and the wishes of millions, that man *is* the most dangerous animal. It's just that some men, like me, are more dangerous. We hunt the biggest game, the most protected, running circles around those who naïvely think we give a Sumatran monkey rat's ass about their rules.

My name is Brett Russell. I am a *most* dangerous animal.

***

I know where to look because rare beasts are often the dangerous ones, and the dangerous ones are those that receive the most ink. When I read in "News of the Weird" or *El Miami Herald* about vulnerable villagers living right along a riverbank on the Amazon reporting lost children who would never wander or linger at the waterline, vanished animals as large as llamas, and even seen wooden fishing boats broken into pieces to get at an open bucket of bait, that's when I know something big—a ravenous crocodile or even an anaconda, which can reach 26 feet long and 325 pounds in weight—is just asking to be bagged and tagged. Exotic species, perhaps, ones protected by laws that no one losing children gives a damn about.

Ever hear of Iquitos, in Peru? It's the largest populated area in the world not accessible by any road. It's either airplane or boat if you want to visit. Why the hell you would want to visit Iquitos is beyond me, but I don't get to choose the places I hunt—money does. I just go.

Its residents are largely uneducated, highly superstitious (as many Catholic South Americans are), and when their prayers and attempts at protection inevitably fail, they mythologize it into a monster "known" to inhabit that area—a *cryptid*, in science-speak. This is how I get involved in the situation, because I keep my eyes out for any rumor of a cryptid terrorizing an indigenous village.

My man in that part of the Amazon was Jefry, a gangly Peruvian whom I had personally seen take down a murumuru palm tree using nothing but his outsized hands and feet. I contacted him and he told me the Iquitos villagers, some of the poorest on the continent, had reported to police and Army personnel (often the same people in Peru) that a *Yemisch*—essentially an elephant-sized, carnivorous, huge-taloned sloth; I looked it up—was disemboweling animals, eating the meat quickly and leaving the disgorged entrails of its victims in the mud or floating in the river. At least one 5-year-old child had reported being chased by something exactly matching the cryptid's description.

"What do you think, Jef?" I asked in Spanish after I came down the steps of the charter plane at Vignetta International Airport and the attended put my heavy bags on the tarmac.

It was cool early morning, the sun just peeking over the horizon, but it was already humid as hell. "We got a *Yemisch* here or what? One of their heads would look great on the wall of a man cave."

Jefry laughed. "Whatever it is, it's a monster, Mister Russell. Something comes out of the river and steals goats and dogs and tries to eat small children. Then it drags them into the river and … does what it does, you know."

"Sounds a lot like a crocodile to me."

"You always say that." He popped the locks on the Range Rover and we got in.

"I always say it because that's what it usually is," I said, taking out a cheroot and reaching for the Rover's lighter, which had been switched out for a sleek doohickey of some kind connected to Jefry's iPad tucked between the seats. "Where's the goddamn lighter?"

Jefry laughed again. "Nobody uses the lighter as a lighter anymore, *amigo*. It's a 120-volt power outlet now. Look, you can keep your electronics charged even as—"

"Yeah, whatever. You got an app on there that lights cheap cigars?"

"You come four thousand miles and don't bring a match?"

Five minutes from the airport and the road was already crap. This was going to be a fun drive. I said, "I got matches in my checked bags—you can't bring that shit as carry-on onto an airplane anymore, dude."

Jefry looked at me with incredulity. "You got two .338 high-powered Winchester Magnums in your luggage!"

"You can't light a cigar with a rifle, *el jefe*." Oh, wasn't I just so hilarious? "Anyway, I brought five, since we have three hunters. But again, try to bring those in your carry-on for a commercial flight from Denver to Lima. Same thing with matches and lighters. And hair gel over 3 ounces. All of it goes into the checked bags."

Once again, my Peruvian friend guffawed. "So how come you didn't get a pack of matches at the airport just now?"

"Number one, that Quonset hut barely had a telephone, let alone traveler's conveniences," I said, then leaned in close and crooked my finger for him to bring his ear closer. I whispered, "And number two, cars are supposed to have *lighters* stuck in their lighter holes, not Steve Jobs' goddamn *pene*."

Jefry never really stopped laughing this whole time, even when he reached over, popped the glove compartment, and pointed to a full Bic *encendedor* right there. I smiled despite myself and grabbed it to light the end of my cheroot.

I couldn't wait to get my trusty, totally dangerous book of *non-safety* matches out of my bags and stick them into their familiar place in my back pocket. Lots of room back there anyway, since I don't carry a wallet—the shit I do and the places I do it, my money and papers are always in a discreet, flat vinyl pouch hanging from my neck.

We hit a huge pothole and I almost set my hair on fire as we lunged forward. "God, I hate the roads in Peru."

"That's Iquitos, man. You got a car here, you brought it by boat. Only the richest people have cars."

"You're rich?"

He smiled. "*La organización* makes sure we get what we need, *no*?

"*Sí, muchacho.*" I thought of the more than $25,000 worth of weapons and two full stocks of different ammunition for each, every rifle sitting in its own rugged, foam-insulated case. The commercial and then charter flights to Iquitos for myself and the three merry hunters. Supplies for as much as a 10-day hunt, since crocs don't just offer themselves up to grab bait like sharks do. Bribes to local officials to look the other way. All paid for by what

Jef called "The Organization," which was the right way to refer to it, nice and anonymous, since what we were doing was unbelievably illegal and plausible deniability an essential quality.

"This ain't a big driving town, man. You're lucky we're even *on* a road."

"Yeah, my ass feels totally blessed," I mumbled around my cheroot as we nearly careened into another monster hole in the asphalt. "So who's on Team Killer Croc this time?"

"You mean killer *cryptid*, man." The word sounded funny inserted into his Spanish: *creepteed*. "One of these days, it's going to be *not* a crocodile and you are going to feel very stupid for making assumptions in the jungle."

I had worked with Jefry in South America ten times over the past couple of years, and every time it was a croc which went feeding on pets and children in the villages encroaching on their habitat. *Every* time. "Okay, who's on Team Monster From Outer Space this time?"

Jefry almost drove off the "road" from laughing so hard. "No one has ever proven the *Yemisch* not to exist," he was able to say once he got his breath. "*Pero sí*, our hunters are expecting it to be a big crocodile."

"Yeah, they wouldn't know a *Yemisch* if it bit them in the ass," I said with a smile, but my joke apparently didn't translate well. (In English, that gag kills.) "Anyway, how big are we talking here?"

"That little kid who got away? He said the *Yemisch* stopped chasing him once it noticed a goat tethered to a post. He said it took two bites—one to rip the goat off the rope into its mouth and one to swallow. That is a *big* croc, Mister Russell."

"Stop calling me that."

"No."

I love working with Peruvians—they give and take no bullshit whatsoever and are funny as hell. So I shrugged and said, "The kid reported it as a giant sloth, too. How much are we going to rely on his eyewitness testimony?"

"All I'm saying is the hunters are expecting probably to be hunting a Black Caiman."

As I mulled this over, the Range Rover got into Iquitos proper. The road was getting a little better, but not by much.

"Those are endangered," Jefry added, unnecessarily.

"That's why we're here, *amigo*." I had smoked the cheroot down to a stub, which I tossed out the window. I used the Bic to light another one. "To assist the goddamn Nautilus-machine–fit dentists and lawyers. White men more likely to get eaten by a crocodile than to bag it themselves."

"I do not know this 'Nautilus machine.' Is it for diving?"

Now I chuckled, looking at the sinewy muscles on my companion's bare arms. "I'm too embarrassed for my race to even explain it."

"So this is a joke, like the electric clothing dryer?"

"That wasn't a joke, Jef. That's something in almost every North American home. It heats the air while it …" I couldn't think of the Spanish word for *tumble*. "… throws your clothes around in a circle."

He snorted and said, "*Claro, claro.*" ("Of course, of course," as in "Pull the other one.")

"Anyway, let's make sure these guys have the right rifles and ammo before they go shooting at a floating tree stump, or each other."

"That's why they book you, right? Lead them right to the where the crocodile is bothering people so they can shoot it and feel like big men, saving the village or some shit?"

"Yep," I said in English. I had an ad running in nearly every hunting and rifle magazine, always a small, text-only piece all the way in the back. It read:

> DON'T LET "THEM" TELL YOU WHAT TO HUNT
>
> Experienced guide available. I know what wild species are endangered: crocodiles, elephants, tigers, etc. Contact me if you need to see these animals yourself so you know exactly what animals are RARE and the government says NOT to

hunt. Inquiries to Box ES-338 % this
publication.

I place the ad every month in print magazines and that's how
these "tough guys" find me. The mags put their classifieds on the
Internet, so the ad can be found online as well, but never with
anything identifying me like putting up my own Web page would
do. (Also, I hate computers.) They know the shooting and killing
and such is their job—mine is only to get them near enough to pull
that trigger. Of course, Jefry and I enlist these rich would-be
Hemingways to rope and then immobilize the animal (big cats are,
perhaps counter-intuitively, the easiest to keep still, and the good
old crocodiles among the toughest and take multiple men to
handle), but then it's all them. They envision themselves as heroes,
saving the encroaching human community from this animal,
technically "endangered" but really, when they think about it,
more of a danger itself.

And that makes it all right, I suppose.

\*\*\*

The Amazon River is huge. *Huge*. It is wide and deep. No one
knows all the creatures that live in these waters, but pretty much
everyone knows it's chock-full of things that want to eat you,
infect you, or kill you in some other way. There are piranha,
worms that old explorers say want to crawl up your urethra,
mosquitoes that *definitely* want to give you malaria, there's
leprosy, all sorts of good stuff available.

If there were such a thing as the *Yemisch*, it wouldn't be any
less likely than a lot of weird shit that the Amazon is actually
confirmed as having. Other than the Congo in deepest, darkest
Africa, the Amazon is home to more mysterious and dangerous
zoological discoveries than any place on Earth.

But the dentist, the urologist, and the Toyota dealership owner,
each of whom found me through my classified ad and wired
$50,000 to a front account to hunt with me, had probably never
heard of a *Yemisch* and wouldn't have cared even if it *did* exist.
No, they were here to bag the enormous and deadly Black Caiman
crocodile—ideally three, one for each of them—an animal that had

been hunted right to the edge of extinction into the 1970s for its handbag and shoe-enhancing hide. The species had rebounded since then, only lately to fall to low numbers again because of encroachment by the explosive growth of the human population and their desire to grow, eat, and sell land-consuming crops.

It was my job, and Jefry's, to lead these rich fellows right to the crocs, which as always I figured to be where the supposed *Yemisch* attacks were reported. I brought the guns and hunting prowess, Jefry brought his unequaled knowledge of the mighty Amazon, and our three clients paid their money to have a rifle placed in their hands and be told where to shoot. (All strictly confidential, of course, because poaching an endangered species in a place like the Amazon basin, where ecotourism is sometimes the only thing supporting the economy, can get you in big, *big*, bigger-than-a-*Yemisch* trouble with the law.)

To help protect the guilty, I will call the dentist "Dan"; the Toyota guy "Theodore"; and the urologist "Peter." (*Ha!* I crack myself up.) Jefry and I met them at the Arandú Bar, a colorful tavern overlooking the river. We would soon be headed down to the Bélen District, located at the southern tip of Iquitos and one of the poorest areas of the city, where the attacks were occurring and where my clients expected to welcomed as heroes there to save the children. And the goats and such. But first things first.

Dentist Dan was tanned so evenly he looked like a cartoon. He was in great shape—muscled arms, flat stomach, bulging quads— each muscle looking *exactly* as if it were exercised individually under the supervision of an expensive personal trainer. He shook my hand with the intent to crush it but was well met by my manly manliness. We didn't technically take out a ruler to compare dicks, but it worked as a proxy fight and ended in a draw anyway.

Toyota Ted had a hell of a belly and was puffy in the face and bloated in the neck, the way a middle-aged former high school football star gets after he's extremely comfortable financially and the first wife who plopped out his three children is shoved aside for a younger model. His handshake revealed pudgy, smooth hands. *Absolutely* what you want when you're going after an 800-pound, 13-foot-long beast that's half teeth and the other half even more dangerous as the muscle-bound animal feels cornered and starts thrashing.

Peter the Penis Poker was thin as a rail and looked like a "before" picture in a muscle magazine ad. He sported a lip-shadow pencil moustache and his fingers felt like spider's legs as they wrapped around my hand at our greeting. I was glad when that contact was over.

We all sat in a curved booth and the skinny native *camarera* brought the group some beers even though it was just 8 in the morning. I guess that's what they expect *gringos* up and about just after sunrise in Iquitos would want, and it wasn't wrong. This suited us just fine.

"So you're the guy who knows where the, ah ..." Dan said in English but still in a low voice, looking around the empty bar before continuing, "... where the *big game* is?" He said "big game" like we were using codewords, not really a bad decision considering how hard Peru had come down on poachers in recent years.

(*Don't mess with tourist money* could have been the slogan of the new Peru, especially in its cities along the Amazon. To poor countries that depended on tourism, poaching was *literally* stealing vital national resources. But wasn't that why one became rich in the first place? To take what you want, whether others want to give it to you or not? These *muy rico* "big game" hunters wanted crocodile heads as their trophies. They hired me—and I hired Jefry—to get them what they wanted.)

"Funny you say that," I said, leaning in to enhance that secret-men's-club vibe, "because the village we're going to? They're lost dozens of animals and even small children to this monster." So I did fib a little on the "small children" part, but guys like this trio liked to add righteousness to their technically illegal activities, making them feel like vigilantes working above cold, uncaring national laws.

"They think it's a *Yemisch*," Jefry said in his perfect but heavily accented English. "That's a, um ... eh, how do you call *amfibio*— oh, yes, amphibious! It is a legendary *amphibious* creature that stalks the river's edge, looking for victims." The would-be poachers looked both entertained and a bit shocked.

I tugged on Jefry's shirt sleeve, trying literally to pull him back. "It's a crocodile. Jef likes to act like he's hunting Bigfoot when it's really just a bear. Of course, bears are dangerous as hell, but they're not a magical creature like Sasquatch or the *Yemisch*."

We all had a chuckle over that, Jefry included. This was part of our shtick, the credulous native guide and the more practical—and white—American hunter.

"No, boys, I'll bet you ten thousand dollars that what we have here is a Black Caiman, the biggest and most dangerous crocodile in the Western Hemisphere. It'll eat any kind of animal it can crush with its jaws—adult humans as well as children included—and swallow it in two bites. There have been numerous reports of animals and children gone missing near the same time, when one Caiman would still be digesting, so I'm thinking there's enough crocs to go around for each of you."

They liked that. Dan, Theodore, and Peter each grinned and practically slapped one another on the back at this news. They came from different parts of the country—Minnesota, New Jersey, and California, I believe—but seem to have bonded on their flight from Peru to the little airport in Iquitos. This was a good thing: they would likely have one another's backs when it came down to it. Probably not—we are an "every man for himself" group of people, poachers and those who help them get to their targets—but maybe. Every little bit of camaraderie would certainly help to keep these guys from accidentally shooting one another ... or Jefry and me.

"All right, gentlemen," I said with a now-serious mien, "tell me what you know about hunting something that weighs more than the three of you put together. Something that wants to kill *you*. Something that could get you twenty years in Peruvian prison if you're caught.

"I ask this because we can't screw this up. There are people in this village, and while they'll be thrilled to have the man-eater gone, stories can start spreading. We will need to hunt, kill and dress each Caiman in the light of day, then smuggle each one into the vehicle and down to the airport. Once you're in the air, you're golden. The U.S. doesn't give a shit what trophies you bring home—some airlines do, but you were warned against flying on those.

"So what do you know? Help Jef and me help you get these monsters." I looked at Dentist Dan to start.

"You gotta shoot them in the head," he said with rock-hard confidence. "Go for the brain. It's tiny, but a body shot isn't gonna do shit except make it mad or make it jump in the water and swim away."

"Can't we just have a boat on hand to chase it?" Peter offered in a reedy voice probably developed by trying to talk with his mouth mostly shut while examining man-parts all up close in his face. "I mean, you follow a lion if you've got an arrow in him, right? Eventually he gets tired and you take him down with another arrow or a bullet to the head."

"Have you done that shit? That's wild," Ted said to Peter, who looked even smaller and mealier under the fat man's gaze.

"Yes. Kind of."

"Kind of? What's 'kind of'?"

Peter cleared his throat weakly and said, "Well, I did wound it and track it, and then I did put it down when it tired from the chase, but it was actually an, um … a cassowary."

"A what, now?"

"It's like an emu," Peter said with his eyes fixed down on the table, "only smaller. I had to go to Australia to bag one of them once the guide showed me where the habitat was."

Ted outright laughed and Dan smiled, looking like he was trying with all his might to suppress it. Jefry looked confused. So it was up to me to rescue the Great Hunter from himself: "Cassowaries are fast sons of bitches, guys—they can run at 30 miles an hour. And if they kick you—"

"They can disembowel a man with the claws on their feet," Peter answered. "They're considered the most dangerous bird in the world."

I wanted to say something like "Pelican supporters may find that insulting," but kept my jocularity to myself. Instead I said, "The main point we should take from Peter here, I think, is that hunting a cassowary is *beyond* illegal in Australia. So he has experience in taking some rare game down, smuggling it past customs, and mounting it for his man cave." I smiled and nodded at Peter, who looked even paler now.

"I, um, didn't actually kill it," he said. "I did shoot at it! But it ran away. It would have been a *definite* kill if I had hit it, though."

"Oh," I said, trying to make it sound like an affirmation instead of an awkward interjection. I failed.

The table was as quiet as a deer blind. Thank god for cute waitresses.

"*¿Más cervezas?*" she asked with a cute dimple in her smile.

We shouted "*¡Sí!*" as one, making her almost jump in surprise. That made her laugh, which made all of us laugh, including Peter.

I literally sighed a breath of relief and said with a renewed smile, "How about you, Doctor Dan? Do you have some helpful experience we should know about?"

Dan leaned back against the vinyl booth with a dentist's grin, all perfectly straight teeth that were whiter than the population of Vermont. He looked at each of his with that smile, bronzed skin crinkling around his eyes, then took a quick look around to make sure no one was near enough to overhear, before he spoke.

"I don't know if it's helpful, but I've brought down 'protected' animals on three—no, four—continents," he said, actually making air quotes when he said "protected."

The other two men looked suitably awed. Jefry and I looked at each other, I think each to use the other as a mirror and make sure we each looked as equally (and falsely) impressed as the other. "That's a hell of a résumé," I said at last.

The crinkles deepened as Dan's blinding grin grew even wider. He counted off the continents on his fingers as he continued: "North America. I went down to the Everglades with an Indian guide, maybe a Seminole who didn't get in on the casino gravy train or whatever, but before I found a Florida Panther, there were about a hundred estimated to live in the wild. After I saw it, there were ninety-freakin'-nine."

This guy was *audacious*. Everybody, myself included, was loving it. The waitress dropped off our fresh beers and gave me a wink. Oh, I felt manly as hell right then, let me tell you.

He continued: "Then you got Asia, goddamned *China*, right? You know what they do to hunters who bag one of their precious pandas? They get *the death penalty*. But that didn't stop me—why would it? A man's got to hunt if he's going to eat that day. I mean, I had high-calorie protein bars and stuff, but that's the reason behind allowing a man to hunt: he needs that animal for meat, warmth, and so on. I could only take the head with me—hard to smuggle out a 250-pound carcass, even on a private charter flight—but that's the solid reason we all hunt. You guys get me.

"Anyway, I got the right grease onto the right palms and there I was, staring at one of these majestic black-and-white creatures munching on some bamboo and *pow!*" Dan mimed shooting a rifle as he said this, then added with a laugh, "I have to keep *that* trophy in my study at home, goddamn *yakuza* or whatever would come looking for me if I had it on display.

"Africa, nailed an elephant—got the tusks in my living room—and then in Australia? You'll love this. In Australia, I bagged a protected rhino that they had relocated from South Africa to save it!" He banged the table as he roared with laughter at that, the others joining in.

Jefry and I exchanged a covert glance and I made a mental note to give Dan the most powerful, special rifle, since he lived up to the Internet research we had done on him: he was frickin' *serious* about his hunting, and had developed his skills like a master.

The others, not so much.

Theodore of Toyota Town said, "I can't match any of that stuff. I mean, I've gotten deer and such in season, but this is my first … um, *real* hunting trip."

He got slaps on the back and gestures of support from his two fellow poachers. Jefry and I just watched.

"All right, then. I was looking for anything you guys knew specifically about hunting crocodiles, but no worries. We'll head out this morning," I said, looking at my waterproof and shockproof diving watch, "because the heat of the day is the only time you're going to find a Caiman sunning itself on the riverbank. It's relaxed and, most importantly, *out of the water.* If you try to wrestle a croc in the water, you're doomed.

"But let's say we find one sunning itself. Peter is right that you go for a headshot, because that will usually immobilize them. But the killshot is *here*"—I indicated the base of my skull—"where it's little brain is. Otherwise, shooting them only makes them slip back into the water and disappear."

Everybody nodded sagely. We ate breakfast, loaded the poachers' gear into the SUV, then drove through the slums of Bélen to start *two* hunts: They had theirs and I had mine, and the twain were about to meet.

\*\*\*

All five of us got outfitted with shoulder GoPro cameras—an edited video of the hunter's triumphs was included in the package price— and we set the three men in different spots along the river, giving each instructions to hide in the bodacious flora and watch for a Black Caiman (or any croc) to come out of the muddy water to get warm in the sun. Crocodiles need to do this to keep their temperature high enough, since they're cold-blooded—O, the irony—and a nap in the blazing South American sun kept them going through the day and chilly nights in the water.

Dan, Ted, and Peter were each in sight of the others, rifles wrapped in towels on the mud and walkie-talkies in their hands to alert everyone of any potential targets, but Jefry and I convened just out of view and out of earshot to discuss our own hunt.

"If I went on a hunt that took ten days, I'd need a good divorce lawyer," Jefry joked quietly in Spanish.

"I said it *might* take *up to* ten days. Besides, that's to bag an Amazon crocodile. We don't need to wait that long," I said, and checked my sidearm to make sure it was loaded and the safety was on. Jefry did the same with his weapon, or whatever the correct procedure was with *a freaking crossbow*. I laughed as quietly as possible and said to Jefry, "What the hell is *that?*"

He did his best to look like his male pride was under attack. "This is *muy macho*, my white brother. It intimidates. It also delivers a shot that can pierce a crocodile's hide to get at that tiny *cerebro*."

"We're not hunting crocodiles."

He looked at the highly, lovingly polished wood of his weapon and smiled. After a moment of admiration, he said, "This works even better against people. They see a gun, they know in their minds it's a gun and they could die. But they see ol' *la ballestai* here, man, they *see* that arrow pointing at their neck or their gut … they don't know if they'll die, but they know that whatever happens, it's going to *hurt*."

We both grinned at that truth, but then came the unmistakable *crack* of a rifle shot.

I had my walkie-talkie to my mouth in less time than it took me to round the corner of foliage and see Peter the Pecker-Checker standing on the bank with his weapon pointed at a spot in the water. "*Stand down!*" I shouted as I stomped toward the skinny poacher. "What the hell are you doing, man?"

"I saw one!" he said, still looking gleeful but also confused at my anger. "I could see a little yellow blob in the water right after I shot. It must be fat or something, right, oozing out of the wound? I really think I might have hit him. "

"I really think I might hit *you*, you dumb son of a bitch," I snarled before remembering we had to be *quiet* in order to lull a Caiman into climbing up onto the mud. In a much-lowered voice I said, "What happened to waiting until one came out, then alerting Jef and me, so we can make sure you do this shit correctly?"

Peter's set his weak chin and puffed up his concave chest in defiance. "I paid a lot of money for this—I'm going to do it *my* way. *I* am the hunter here. You're just my backup."

I said to Jefry in Spanish, "I think I see what went wrong on the emu hunt." Spanish for "emu" is "*emú*," so to prevent Peter figuring out what I was saying, I used "*avestruz*," the word for "ostrich."

"What are you saying? Hey, I paid you—you speak English so I know what you're saying."

The other two men had walked silently up behind Jefry and me. They didn't say anything in support of their comrade when we turned to see them there, but they didn't seem to disagree with him, either.

"Ted, Dan, I'm right, right? Fifty thousand dollars means we can hunt however we want, right? Back me up here, guys."

Ted mumbled noncommittally, scratching his belly and looking down at the mud.

Dan gave Peter a hard stare and said as calmly as possible, "We paid these men to help us bag giant crocodiles. We have to follow their advice if we want the kill."

Jefry and I nodded, trying to agree with Dan while not making Peter feel like the assclown he obviously was. "I'm just trying to help y—" I said, stopping short as something caught my eye several hundred yards behind the game-hunting urologist.

Peter must have seen the look in my eye, because he pivoted 180 degrees in the mud to look at whatever I was looking at. In seconds, all of us saw a huge crocodile—*huge*, like 14 feet and almost half a ton of ravenous predator—creeping out of the water and onto the bank. It stopped before going into the jungle. It was sunning itself.

Peter whipped his rifle up and would have pulled the trigger if I hadn't slapped the safety on before Peter could get his eye against the scope. Then he *did* pull the trigger, but of course nothing happened. I whispered *and* shouted in his ear, "DO *NOT* FIRE!"

"We're too far away for a decent shot," Jefry added in his own whisper.

When I forced Peter's rifle down and turned to instruct the others, Dentist Dan was gone. I started to say "Where did—" but then I saw the muddy bootprints Dan left behind as he stealthily made his way to the riverbank opposite the sunning croc, where the best shot would be. Except now the animal was perpendicular to the water from crawling out and stopping, there was no angle to fire off either a stopping shot *or* a killshot.

I brought the walkie-talkie up to my mouth as slowly as I could and pressed the red button. "Come in, Dan. This is Brett. *Hold your fire*. You're just going to piss it off from that position. Do you read me?"

As slowly as I had gotten my walkie-talkie in position, so did Dan look at the rest of us and hold up his own. Not up to his mouth, but all the way up so we could make no mistake about what it was. He then brought it back down and pitched it like a softball into the Amazon. Then he raised his middle finger to us.

The Caiman—and that is definitely what this beast was, a Black Caiman that was snatching animals and scaring the villagers into thinking it was the mythical *Yemisch* come for their children—

noticed the *plop* in the water and used its short legs to turn 90 degrees to see what, if any, danger was being posed. It noticed *Dan.*

I could hardly believe that an actual crocodile of any kind, let alone this monster, had come out of the water as if on cue. I've waited a week for my party to see one, and half the time it slipped back into the water once it heard any activity. Luckily for us, however, this one had gotten up the bank on the opposite side of the river and wouldn't be spooked away so easily.

"Call the evac copter," I whispered to Jefry. "Get it out here *now* or we're going to have a serious mess on our hands."

Jefry immediately switched the band on his walkie-talkie to summon the waiting helicopter from the airport five and a half miles away. (Over half an hour by car, but three minutes by chopper. That's why we had an airlift on standby, to get where we were *now*, before somebody could die.)

Dan was taking his time—I could see now how he had killed so many skittish and rare creatures. He was fluid in his movements, and even how he tossed the walkie-talkie into the water was calculated to make just enough noise to make the Caiman move but not flee back into the water. It was impressive, but the animal was on the other side of *the Amazon River.* We had no boat to cross and it was too deep to wade through. You couldn't swim across without soaking your rifle, and even if you could, the whole reason we were in Iquitos was that this stretch of the river had an abundance of *man-eating goddamn crocodiles* in it.

Dan checked his footing in the mud and braced himself for the recoil from the loaded rifle I had given him. He very slowly raised the rifle.

I could hear the helicopter now, homing in on my GPS signal.

Dan very carefully lifted the weapon so the scope met his eye, and he aimed slowly, so slowly. I wondered why he even needed my services. Of course, killing an endangered animal was one thing; smuggling it home was quite another.

*Chopchopchopchopchop*, the 'copter getting louder every second. Soon it would be visible over the—

*KAPOW!* Peter's rifle went off. My ears rang like he had put his bullet through my eardrums.

# CHAPTER 2

Unlike Dan, Peter hadn't taken the time to set himself and aim carefully before he took a potshot at the crocodile. He fell back into the mud like a cartoon … but somehow his shot was true.

*Bink!* A small yellow spatter appeared on the center of the croc's body. The giant animal started forward a foot or two, but otherwise remained motionless. Waiting.

"What the hell? Peter, crocs have yellow blood?" Theodore spurted, and raised his rifle and shot without even aiming at all. *Bink!* A splotch of green pocked the Caiman's hide. I was amazed—these morons were crack shots or extremely lucky ones.

"And *green?*"

Peter seethed from where he sat in the mud. "No, they don't," he said, and pointed his rifle directly at my chest.

"Whoa, *whoa!*" Ted shouted, and tried to get his footing enough to knock Peter's weapon aside. He couldn't do it fast enough, though, and Peter squeezed off another round.

*POW!* A splash of yellow exploded against my camos, stinging like a bitch at this distance.

"These are *paintball guns*," Peter said in disgust.

Theodore looked at me like I had just slapped his mother. He raised his own rifle.

*POW!* Now a green pellet from his rifle struck me point-blank and painfully, popping against my jacket. Both men now dropped their hugely expensive paintball-modified rifles into the mud like they were ten-dollar Nerf guns and moved toward me, murder in their eyes.

I hadn't noticed before how Ted's bulk looked awfully muscular under the fat. Or how much Peter resembled a sweaty tweaker about to pull out a switchblade.

I put my hands out. "Okay, fellas, just calm down," I started, but was interrupted by a big fist slamming into my jaw. I spun and fell to the mud on my back, then raised myself up onto my elbows to try to get up before I received more abuse. I brought my teeth together and clacked a few times to make sure they were still in my mouth. I could tell that I had come within a chin hair of getting my jaw broken. "Ted, Peter—"

Now Peter hissed, "Son of a bitch!" and kicked me in the hip while I was prone in the mud. Who kicks a person in the *hip*? Peter, obviously, and while it may have been a weird choice, it was a good one—it hurt like holy hell and made me *yelp* as I brought myself up on all fours and then stood before either of them could kick me in the head.

"Who *are* you, anyway?" Ted grumbled at me as he came in for another shot. "Greenpeace? PETA? Goddamn ASPCA—"

*Whoomp!* He didn't complete his thought, being interrupted by my boot heel slamming into his breadbasket. He wheezed and fell into the muddy bank, his head almost striking the water. He was lucky no crocodile was waiting for a splash to find his next meal.

At least, not yet.

Now Proctologist Peter lunged at me, trying to tackle me and bring me down like I was John Elway at Mile High. But I had the weight advantage and stopped him cold—making my bruised hip scream out in shock—but the little weasel unleashed Plan B and reached up and yanked on my goddamn *balls*.

I retched but kept enough of my wits to bring my knee up to his chin with a sharp *crack* that shut off his lights like I had kicked a pasty-faced switch. He stayed where he fell. I made sure his oxygen paths were clear of mud before doubling over and puking my breakfast and most of last night's dinner right on the back of his head.

I didn't have much chance to enjoy my new artwork before I saw that Theodore has gotten the wind back in his system and was marching toward me like a Sherman tank. Enough was enough now—I pulled my gun from its holster under my jacket and leveled it at Ted's face. "All right, time to—"

The big man slapped the gun out of my hand like it was a toy— even paintballs could have partially blinded him or broken a cheekbone at point-blank range, and these were for-real bullets in my weapon—and grabbed the front of my jacket, yanking me up for a headbutt or maybe to bite off my nose. My feet left the ground.

And stayed there as Theodore froze, a loaded crossbow pointing its arrow tip right at the center of his eyeball. "Put my friend down, *pendejo*, and put your hands up."

The big man returned me to the ground as gently as a snowflake falling, his unmoving gaze fixed on Jefry's crossbow. He put his hands behind his head and plopped down onto his knees when Jefry told him to. Still green but so happy not to have a cracked skull, I moved Ted's hands to behind the small of his back and fastened plastic restraints around his wrists.

This was when Peter made his move, apparently having awakened during our defeat of his fellow poacher. With a thin but loud yell, he barreled right at Jefry, who whipped that magical goddamn crossbow right into his face.

"Back off, *estupido*," he said through bared teeth.

Peter, transfixed with terror at the crossbow and arrow, knelt down and assumed the position as I cuffed him as well.

I said to Jefry, nodding at his medieval weapon, "I'm man enough to admit when I'm wrong. Now let's go get—"

I was cut off by two things happening simultaneously:

One, so "in the zone" was Dentist Dan that he had taken no notice whatsoever of the fight a hundred yards away. No, the dedicated, maybe obsessed, hunter had kept his aim on the Black Caiman, even though the huge animal had jumped forward a bit at each paintball strike. Now, his patience rewarded, he squeezed the trigger on *his* expensive-as-hell modded rifle and a *SHOOP!* sounded simultaneously with the giant croc rocking like a ship hit by a wave. It started to move toward getting back into the water, but the tranquilizer dart Dan's rifle had delivered must have hit the animal right in the nerve bundle behind the skull.

A perfect shot, I had to admit. But Dan, the poacher with the most experience, could tell the difference between a *pow* and a *shoop* coming out of his weapon. He immediately held it out and looked at it with confusion, then consternation … then anger. He yanked open the magazine and, I knew, saw that it was loaded not with the hollow-point, high-power ammunition he expected, but with tranq darts weighted to keep them on target like real bullets and to make the weapon feel as heavy as it would if it were loaded with real cartridges.

Boy, he was *not* happy. He glared at Jefry and me, chucked the $10,000 rifle into the river, and started toward us like the two of us were 12-point bucks ready to be field-dressed and our meat put into coolers. To extend my hunting metaphors into the culinary realm, our geese would have been cooked if the second thing didn't happen at the exact same time that he was examining his traitorous weapon.

That second thing was the five-seater helicopter, the same that had ferried the three would-be poachers from Peru to Iquitos, finally appearing over the tops of the trees and into full view. The black chopper, that had no doubt looked extremely cool to the hunters the evening before, now looked sinister, especially as the pilot and his armed front-seat passenger—our guys from the start—set down right between the stomping Dan and the rest of our party. Fatty and skinny remained cuffed on their knees in the mud, but both managed to sneak confused glances at the helicopter's arrival.

"We just shot the croc," Ted said. "How'd the pickup get here so fast?"

Peter rolled his eyes. "It's not a pickup for the croc, dumbass," he seethed, then looked with fury at me. "It's a pickup for *us*."

I grinned. "Give that man a dollar! You're gonna need it for the Coke machine in prison."

The chopper pilot jumped out and ordered Dentist Dan to the ground, his AK-47 probably *not* loaded with paintballs or sleepy-time darts. Like his two fellows, Dan sank to his knees and put his hands behind his head, but that didn't stop our pilot from continuing to shout. Maybe reading him his rights, if they did that in Peru. Maybe explaining what he was in trouble for. Maybe just saying things to hurt the hunter's feelings, I don't know. But I enjoyed seeing the fit and tan poacher dentist getting reamed, then cuffed and led our way.

The chopper passenger, a tower of muscle wrapped in flak gear that read *WWF*, came our way with his own Kalashnikov, keeping it pointed at the two poachers even though they had been neutralized. Then he lowered his weapon, trapped me in a bear hug and shook Jefry's hand. We had worked in tandem for almost a decade and relied on each other, but I still knew him only by his moniker "The Punisher" (the stylized skull on the front of his vest showing the inspiration), and he knew me only as "Brett Russell," my operational pseudonym.

We always kept our identities secret, even from one another, because "plausible deniability" was essential when we were poaching poachers, seeing as how our clientele was made up of pissed-off rich Americans who would be most interested in dispensing *lots* of revenge when they got out of Peruvian prison. (Peru liked to hold on to its foreign prisoners for transgressions committed on their soil. I admired that.)

The pilot had walked Dan over to us and planted him in the mud, hands cuffed behind his head the same as Peter and Theodore.

The Punisher didn't shout at them the way the pilot had at Dan, probably because Ted and Peter already looked so cowed and defeated it wouldn't have been any fun. As I unclipped the GoPro cameras labeled with their name of each man (as well as Jefry's and my own), he informed them that they were under arrest for poaching an endangered species, the Black Caiman crocodile.

All three reared up simultaneously, protesting that they had shot with paintballs and Dan with a tranquilizer gun—they hadn't poached anything!

The Punisher chuckled at this, and Jefry and I smiled.

"We have all three of you assholes on GoPro, shooting at *and hitting* the croc," the WWF agent said, then rattled off the charges, telling them to be prepared for a matching charge of traveling over borders to commit each act they were being arrested for: "Intent to poach protected wildlife, conspiracy to poach, attempted poaching, not to mention inflicting injury upon protected wildlife. By the way, thanks for collecting the evidence for us." We wiggled the little cameras and laughed.

"This is entrapment!" Peter said, his temper finally getting the best of him. "They put out an ad in magazines, taking our money and setting up these fake expeditions, and then you arrest *us* for shooting *paintballs*? How about these two sons of bitches stole fifty thousand dollars from each of us! This is *bullshit*. I'll be out of your shit jail and your shit country in twenty-four hours!"

"Rich boy," the Punisher said, "you can bribe the judges in Peru all you want. They wear *hoods* during trials, you know that, right? They'll take the money and still put your ass on ice for twenty-four *years*, not twenty-four hours, and you'll never know which one screwed you over."

"Besides, who exactly *entrapped* you?" the pilot said, warming to the fun. He asked this question with a laugh as he and the Punisher got the men to their feet and shoved them toward the helicopter. Then he indicated Jefry and me with a nod. "Those two other poachers nobody will see on the video we give the court, you mean, the ones who got away?"

All three handcuffed men shot daggers from their eyes at Jefry and me. We waved bye-bye to them as I said to the pilot, "We only have ten minutes or so until the big boy wakes up over there. The airlift gonna make it in time?"

The pilot pantomimed cupping his hand around his ear and said, "I can hear them on their way. They'll find a good new home for Biggie over there, somewhere he won't be tempted by villagers' goats or children." He gave me a thumbs-up, and within a few seconds I, too, could hear the WWF helicopter coming for the croc. (Which was good, because we sure as hell weren't swimming across the river to get to it.)

"*You all work together!* There's going to be a *paper trail!*" Peter squeaked as they loaded him and his compatriots into the chopper.

"We got nothing to do with their organization, Mister Cock Doc. *Nada.* But spend lots of your money on lawyers trying to find us—all we are is poachers, too, as far as anyone can see." I grinned as I said this, then laughed at the looks of despair on the faces of the three mighty hunters as the pilot slid the heavy helicopter door closed.

Before they got in the helicopter themselves—and now I could plainly hear the *choopchopchop* of the crocodile relocation airlift 'copter closing in—the Punisher asked me in a quiet voice, "Didn't you say the feeding evidence showed there were at least *two* crocs picking off animals and maybe little kids from this District?"

I slipped a cheroot out of my front pocket—my too-long-postponed first smoke of the day—and a standard, non-girly, non-

"safety" match out of my back pocket. I could scratch it against my stubble, or theirs, or a door frame, anything to make myself look like Joe Frickin' Cool while I lit my little cigar. I clapped my man on the shoulder and said, "Don't you worry. We got two fresh and mighty hunters coming in tomorrow looking to bag themselves a Black Caiman, so I imagine we'll be seeing each other again soon, *el Castigator*."

We laughed. Then the men got back to their black helicopter (waiting for the approaching relocation airlift to safely come in and land on the opposite bank near the sleepy croc) and took off for the Iquitos police headquarters, where the three would be booked and in a week or so shipped off to Lima for a very short trial and very long prison sentences.

As soon as they were out of sight, I turned to my magnificent man in Peru and said in Spanish, "Jef, let's get cleaned up, get some lunch, get you your cut. Then I've got to go pay through the goddamn nose to get those rifles cleaned—or replaced, with that son of a bitch throwing his into the water. We have the whole show again tomorrow."

Jefry laughed at this, nodding at my plan. "But tell you what, *amigo*," he said. "You give me my cut first and *I'll* buy lunch. Save you a little money for your new toys."

\*\*\*

My name is Brett Russell—to anyone who matters, anyway— and I hunt poachers. They are my game and my passion. I'm only sorry that I can't actually shoot them and put their decapitated heads on my wall, maybe set them into some "fierce" position so unlike their actual stances behind desks or selling cars or poking around in people's assholes.

I can't tell you who employs me and Jefry or any of the other associates I work with all over the world. Even if I did tell you, you wouldn't believe it. It's not the World Wildlife Fund or People for the Ethical Treatment for Animals or even the Society for the Prevention of Cruelty to Animals, although I sometimes work closely with those organizations. Just think of me as a free radical floating around in the body of the world, turning into an unrelenting cancer that eats away ivory hunters and rhinoceros-horn traders. I don't care about treaties and agreements between suit-wearing, soft-handed politicos. I care about protecting rare animals from the humans who either go looking for them or find themselves encroaching upon wild areas.

The funny thing—and what infuriates my friends at PETA even as they praise my work—is that I'm also a hunter of animals. I have taken down coyotes in culls in Arizona, shot a huge bear capering near a small town in Idaho, and harpooned a 20-foot, 6,000-pound tiger shark a few miles off the shore of the most popular tourist swimming area in Hawai'i.

Sue me, call me names, whatever, I enjoy hunting. I like to take down other predators. Do I eat the meat, use the bones to make furniture or some shit? No, or in the case of the meat not always (shark flesh is literally soaking in urine the entire animal's life). But I never hunt an endangered animal, a member of a species in proximate danger of vanishing entirely from the Earth. And I never, *ever* hunt for money.

Well, not *never*. The Organization That Will Not Be Named pays me well to hunt poachers, those smug heathens who will drive species to extinction for a fast dollar. But hell, I'd hunt those bastards for free.

# CHAPTER 3

A week after Jefry and I got that second poaching party to shoot at a Caiman—it had taken us three very uncomfortable days of careful stalking to find one—I would have been happy never to see an ounce of mud again for the rest of my life. But I also swore I'd have been happy never to see another blade of long grass after stopping some baddies in the Serengeti; and, if memory serves, after a seemingly endless assignment in dark Siberia that saved two extremely rare Amur tigers and sent four ethnic Mongols to the gallows, I told my boss that I would be ecstatic never to see another goddamn birch tree and even happier never to see another form printed in Russian with English translations so bad I had to assume имя meant "age" and возраст was where I put my birthplace. (My uneducated guesses were rewarded with stern looks and fresh, empty forms.)

Do I feel bad about those Mongols hanging by their necks behind the Yermak Timofeyevich District Court Assembly Building in Tobolsk? Sure, I feel bad at the death of any man, but all operatives like me do is keep them from killing animals they have no business killing—then I turn them over to the authorities and I'm on the next sled to Denver International. I can't say I lose any sleep over the deaths of poachers deep-pocketed enough to hire me to get within rifle shot of a Siberian tiger. These aren't starving children in Sierra Leone stealing chickens to survive—a capital crime there, by the way—but one-percenter men and women (oh, yes, indeed) greasing palms and hiring guides for $50,000 so they can rob the world of its beauty for their own smug enjoyment.

So to hell with them.

Anyway, I sit at a desk in Denver, The Organization's front actually a fully functioning and successful international business. This front company employs four thousand people in Colorado and twice as many in countries west, east, north, south, Capitalist, Communist, Socialist, Muslim, Buddhist, Vegetarian, everywhere.

Can my flights to Peru, to Moscow, to Addis Ababa be traced back to this front corporation? I suppose so, but it flies thousands of employees every year to the furthest corners of the Earth, so singling mine out would be practically impossible even if anyone knew where to look. I am well hidden by The Organization—so even if some angry poacher's family hires a $400-an-hour lawyer who hires a $1,000-a-week private investigator who hires a $25-per-tooth-knocked-out thug to shake down the classified page editors of *Guns and Ammo* or wherever my advertisement appeared to ensnare the unfortunate Great White Hunter in question, the cash used to pay for the ad arrived in an envelope long since discarded.

My desk is one of fifty in the soil of this fertile cubicle farm. I wear a button-down Oxford and tie and (more often than not) wraps and bandages over stitches. I tell my "friends" at the front company that I do extreme sports on the weekends and do rock climbing or some such bullshit when I travel to cool places on the boss's dime. I have no idea what they do—business stuff? TPS reports? Contracts for things?—and they have no idea what I do. Which is use Rosetta Stone to learn whatever tongue I need for my next "business trip," play Hearthstone, research new developments in hunting weaponry, look at the pictures on my cubicle wall, eat lunch, go to meetings covering things I have nothing to do with, look at pictures on my cubicle wall …

When I started with The Organization a dozen years ago, recruited right from Army Special Operations without one bit of paperwork before my second tour was even completed, I put random, anonymous faces into the frames, just something there to make my cubicle look like it belonged to an actual person. Then, not too long after what happened, I took the fake pictures down and shoved them in a drawer. After that, I put the frames back up but put ———'s and ———'s actual photos in them. I put up my 8-year-old's crayon, then colored pencil, drawings of the biggest, fiercest dinosaurs he had read about. I don't remember any of their names except *Tyrannosaurus rex*, but he knew every name and could tell you what they ate, when they lived, and when they vanished from the face of the Earth. I also put up some poems my wife had written to me, ones that make me heartsick now whenever I read them.

I had to remind myself of their faces and what they loved every day. But if they thought I would stop, if they thought it would make me quit, then they were as dumb as they were evil. I told my bosses at The Organization that I was available now any time, to go any place, for whatever duration an operation would take.

So the ones who did what they did to scare me, to stop me? They only made me able to work 24 hours a day at ruining them. A man without a family to come home to can't ever *go* home. His home died when his wife and son died. They couldn't get at me, so they got at *them*.

So who are "they," the people or group of people who killed my family and left little stuffed rhinos and tigers and gorillas next to them to soak up their blood? I don't know—no one ever took credit or followed up with taunting letters to torture me. But every time a poacher cries on his knees in front of me, I know I'm doing the right thing, because my doing *this* was what hurt them. Whoever they were.

But whoever they were knew who *I* was. That I was "Brett Russell" and was endangering something they wanted. Keeping them from money or power or whatever it was that their poaching was supposed to bring them. But I ask myself whenever I'm in the office, looking out at my fellow cubicle dwellers: *How did they know who I am? How could anyone possibly know? And why didn't they just kill me?* I have never been able to see what advantage they could have gained by killing my family, taunting me with the stuffed animals, but not killing *me*.

I've tried to take the detective route and "follow the money," but no matter how much money I cost the bastards—and there are millions upon millions to be made selling parts of nearly extinct animals to China and the Chinese diaspora all over the world, how could they have found me in the first place? Although I've thought about it every single day for eight years, I've never been able to see how they could learn my identity considering the multiple layers of obfuscation The Organization puts between its agents (I assume there are others like me, probably sitting in a cubicle like mine in the front business office) and the rest of the world.

There's never been another incident indicating that anyone knows my non-Brett identity. But one was enough: Now I live and breathe to nail these people, these poachers. I have—and I want—nothing else.

*Ping!* An email message popped up on my desktop, pulling my attention away from the pictures and out of the dead past. It read:

> *Party planning committee meeting*
> *starting immediately. Don't forget to*
> *bring the fun!*

I cracked a smile despite my dark mood. This was my boss—my *real* boss, my Organization boss—and his way of telling me to meet him for a brand-new assignment. The timing on this might have set a new record, considering I had just gotten back from South America less than a week ago.

*Bringing the fun now*, I wrote back and got myself to the elevator, nodding at "co-workers" who probably had completely forgotten I worked there. Which was perfect. Go back to your TPS spreadsheet contract things or whatever. Time for me to save the world again.

In no conspicuous haste, I got up from my desk and walked through the office and around a screen that cut off any view of the hallway I was about to use. I walked past a sign reading "Omega Badges Only Beyond This Point," put there to block anyone who accidentally or purposefully stumbled upon the hidden corridor. The only front business employees who sported an $\Omega$ were the security officers who worked for the front company, thus quelling curiosity about the badge requirement. (In fact, no one else in the front company wore badges or ID cards. Each employee—very well-paid employee, I might add—was "chipped" like a cat adopted from a shelter. This electronic chip is what allowed an employee to enter an "airlock" big enough to contain just one person, where he or she would be allowed to go through the second door to the office once the first behind the employee was shut and reset.)

Once I passed the Omega badge sign, I walked a little further past closed doors to empty offices until I got to the one marked "Janitor." I used a fingerprint-identifier key to open this door and slip into what looked to be a regular broom closet with buckets, mops, and bathroom supplies. At the rear of this small room, obscured by some shelving filled with buckets labeled "industrial cleaner" and other bulky opaque objects, was another door: this was the "executive elevator." It could not be stumbled upon. Anyone finding it was either an authorized operative or a saboteur-*cum*-spy.

I pressed the button for the executive elevator. The doors opened immediately, this phone-booth–sized car not going anywhere except to the level of the building where my boss had his office. Even then, one had to have a second fingerprint-activated electronic key to get the doors to close and the elevator moving. In addition, even if two people, authorized or not, tried to squeeze in, the doors wouldn't close. Like the front-door "airlock," this was a one-person-at-a-time situation. Once the doors did close, an anesthetizing vapor was automatically released, one against which I—and I assume other operatives as well as the Boss himself—had been injected with a chemical defense that needed to be renewed each month. Anyone not thus protected would pass out in seconds, and the elevator doors would automatically reopen in order for The Organization's security team (uniformed exactly like the front business's security team) to remove the unauthorized user and take him or her to God knows what kind of interrogation.

The Boss either never left the office, which was highly unlikely, or he had his own secure elevator (or, hell, a private set of good old-fashioned stairs) for entering and leaving the building. Or maybe he had a helicopter. Or a *Star Trek* transporter. I certainly didn't know, the same way I didn't know the Boss's real name (although he of course knew mine).

This may seem excessive, but there were a hundred damned good reasons for every bit of this expensive and time-consuming security: Not more than one person could enter the office, let alone the executive elevator. This meant no invasions of hostiles, whether terrorists, pro-poaching spies, or misguided government jackboots. It also meant that any miscreant attempting to access The Organization would become lost, get gassed, or "be taken to a second location," something I knew about only by those words but creeped the living hell out of me.

I ran through the gauntlet of security, of course being authorized to use the executive elevator when summoned by the Boss, and the claustrophobia-inducing car rose through an uncounted number of levels to open up on his office suite. His administrative assistant, a Miss ——————, welcomed me with a broad smile, but I knew she had a pedal-activated scattergun which automatically pointed at my heart and would pump me full of radium-rich pellets if somehow it missed the primary mark. (The Boss told me all this. Maybe it was a lie to keep me on my toes, but I don't see why The Organization wouldn't go the extra mile and outfit his secretary with such a weapon.)

I'm sure my body had been x-rayed and scanned eight ways from Sunday on the elevator ride up, and since Miss ————— knew the Boss had summoned me, she brightly indicated that I could enter his office. I returned her sweet smile, never forgetting that she would kill me in an instant if I somehow messed up the protocol. I hadn't yet, and I met with the Boss for a briefing before every new assignment.

I pressed the fingerprint pad (which also measured body temperature, in case some villain cut off an operative's hand to get him through that bit of security, as if he or she would ever make it that far) and the door clicked to allow me ingress.

The Boss was, as usual, at his desk, smoking a cigarette. This was one of the things I loved about his office: I immediately took a fresh match from my back pocket, striking it against the chin of one of his hunting trophies, then lit a fresh cheroot from my front pocket, loving every molecule of the acrid smoke. He motioned to one of the comfortable chairs across from his desk and I sat, sinking a little into the luxury. The chair was upholstered with leather, a strange choice (as were mounted hunting trophies) for an organization seeking to end poaching, but one that made sense in the context of the Boss's office.

"H————," he said with a smile. "Excellent work, as always, on the *Yemisch* down there."

"Thank you, sir." I grinned because I didn't have to remind him that it was an endangered Black Caiman we relocated, not the villagers' bogeyman cryptid. He had my report and was skeptical of chimerical creatures, although he enjoyed regaling me with stories about them.

"You know, H————, you are our number-one operative in the field."

"Thanks, but aren't I the *only* operative in the field?"

His smile was tight, but it was impossible for me to read. This may have been because the Boss had absolutely no hair on his head or anywhere else his skin was visible. His lack of eyebrows kept me from detecting irony or anything else expressible through his smooth forehead. No eyelashes gave him a reptilian look, and his utterly bare head added to the effect. He also wore contact lenses—at least that's what I *think* they were—that made the color of his iris the same as the whites of his eyes. When we first met, I thought maybe he was an albino who was trying to hide it; my other hypothesis was that he was undergoing chemotherapy. But that was twelve years ago and to me, except for slight crow's feet and the usual bodymorphic changes of a face over 12 years, he looked exactly the same. I could only figure he kept himself in this state so he could disguise his identity extremely easily, something important when very rich and angry people would give their all to see you dead.

Finally he said, "You know I can't answer that. Let's say, 'as far as you know.' However, no one else in The Organization has brought down as many bad guys as you have. Let that be a comfort to you in your ignorance of our personnel details."

"It's good to hear, sir. Even though you're a bit of a son of a bitch."

He barked a real laugh at that. He wanted a tough guy when he recruited me from Army Special Ops, and so that's the face I showed him. "Very good," he said, still chuckling. "So I know all about your latest hunt. Do you want to hear about mine?"

I answered as I always did, and it was sincere: "Hell yes, sir."

His expressions may well have been nigh impossible to read, but there was no mistaking the joy and pride he exuded when showing off *his* latest kill. He stood from his chair and I got up as well to follow him into the "trophy room" adjoining his office, feeling a little thrill of excitement *and* anxiety about what he had added to his collection.

The lights in the trophy room were motion-detecting, and so the soothing Edison-bulb lighting brought the dozens of heads attached to fine mahogany mounts into clear view. Also taxidermied animals—none of them endangered, of course—stood in fierce poses, so lifelike it wouldn't have completely surprised me if they moved.

The Boss led me to the back of the room and flicked on a special LED that illuminated the newest piece in his menagerie: mounted on a beautiful and no-doubt rare wood was the head of a Caucasian man with blue eyes (which, like all taxidermied creatures, were glass), an insouciant moustache curled at the ends, and an cheap-looking pipe clenched between his teeth. His skin was tan and his bushy eyebrows fixed him with an expression of eternal brutality.

"Do you like?"

It was not ass-kissing that made me say, "I do, indeed. Do I know who this is?"

"I don't know, H———. Do you?"

Something about the man's face made me think Australian. And the Boss collected only the most valuable and difficult specimens. Who hadn't been showing up on my searches as actively poaching in recent weeks? My mind went round and round for a moment and then I saw the man's face on dossiers and his own bragging Facebook page, where he had most recently posed with his Snow Leopard kill.

"Shit—excuse me, Boss—but is this Rupert C———?"

My Boss actually clapped his hands. "Indeed! Brilliant, isn't he?"

"I don't know if I'd call the son of a whore 'brilliant,' but—"

"No, silly boy, my taxidermist! In life, Rupert smoked the most rare and expensive tobacco pipes in the world, even as he hunted in Nepal. So when he was stretching the skin over the frame, he called and told me he was considering making him smoke a seven-dollar pipe from Wal-Mart in perpetuity! My god, the irony, the *insult*—I love it." And then he spit in the face of Rupert C———, a millionaire in life and now, in death, a custom and illegal taxidermy job that cost one hundred thousand dollars if it cost a penny.

I enjoyed the Boss's trophy room. It was stocked well with the heads of infamous poachers that he had killed himself, or at least *said* he killed himself, Caucasian and darker faces in equal proportion, and I had no reason to doubt him. My favorites were the full-body specimens, which must have been a complete bitch to get through customs without the sender—certainly not the Boss himself, but someone he hired, perhaps an operative like me—identifying himself. He sent the poor men and women back in coffins, "hunting accident" victims who were going home to their families in the United States. And then he had them stuffed.

Did I mention that The Organization is hardcore? It's not in my job description (I mean, if I had one) to know how we are funded, although they don't always pay me directly, my money coming mostly from the poaching assholes. But there were also jobs in which we wouldn't be seeking any poachers, just trying to keep people who lived near the endangered predator threatening their homes from taking things into their own hands, definitely getting themselves killed and possibly the beast in question as well.

We returned to his office and retook our seats. Down to business.

"Tell me: have you ever heard of *Kasai Rex*?"

The question startled me, seeing as how I was just reminiscing at my boy's dinosaur drawings. But the name didn't ring a bell. "Eh … it must have been a larger predator, judging by the 'Rex' in its classification … so I'd say it was a cousin of *T. Rex*," I said, sadly smiling on the inside that my son would have been able to list facts about the damned thing until my Boss begged for mercy.

He laughed and said, "Good guess!" He grabbed a pen out of the pencil cup on his desk, something that was startling no matter how many times I saw it: a hollowed-out and preserved human foot and ankle, done in the style of those elephant feet hunters hollow out for umbrella stands. It didn't take me long to figure out what the soft and sumptuous beige leather of the comfortable chairs was made from, either.

No wonder it was so impossible to get into the Boss's office without his permission—he must have had repurposed parts from 60 different poachers in here. The irony was exquisite, but the authorities might not have found it so amusing. I knew—because he told me, anything I knew about The Organization was from what he told me—that he had the entire office wired to incinerate everything inside should he ever need to rid himself of his trophies in a hurry. (Say, between the time a police detective or FBI agent could get through to the elevator and take it up to the Boss's *sanctum sanctorum*.) He had it set so that it would burn itself out quickly and not endanger anyone else in the building, but only after it reduced to ashes everything within those office walls.

"This is what witnesses have described as coming to eat their children and lay waste to their huts and tents," he said, and showed me what he had been scribbling at: a lizard that looked like a cross between a Tyrannosaurus and a salamander, its arms bigger than a T. Rex and its jaws narrowing at the front. He had also sketched the silhouette of a human next to it for scale.

The human looked quite small.

"So it's another crocodile," I said, a little bored, "reacting to the encroachment on its territory."

"Maybe. Probably *C. porosus*, a saltwater croc that's traveled far from home. But whatever it is, we have reason to believe it is rare and saving and relocating it might be the key to keeping its species alive."

"Obviously, it's not really a dinosaur, so who's calling it *Kasai Rex*?"

He pressed a couple of buttons and a screen descended from the ceiling. Since there were no windows in his bunker/office, there was no natural light to worry about, and when he turned on the computer projector I was instantly treated to a map of the Democratic Republic of Congo. The Boss used a laser pointer to indicate different areas on the map; he was not the kind to stand and make a full dog-and-pony show out of it. Which I appreciated, actually.

"The people calling it *Kasai Rex* are the people working in the Congo diamond mines right next to the Kasai river. Mutterings about the cryptid couldn't stay contained to the poor bastards digging for diamonds with their bare hands in the soft dirt near the river. They told the story to drivers taking the diamonds out— about the children and animals gone, about finding their tents destroyed and food taken."

"Tents? I thought mud-and-grass huts were more the thing out that way."

The Boss smiled at my naïveté. "This isn't a village, H————. The tents are planted there as living quarters for the diamond miners by Vermeulen Corp. These poor shits are hundreds of miles from home in the DRC—"

"I hate calling it that. It's not democratic or a repub—"

"Do not interrupt me, if you please."

Oh, I pleased, all right. I could feel a bead of sweat form on my forehead. I'd rather have a crossbow pointed at my eye than have the Boss fix me with that annoyed glare.

"Call it 'Congo' if you like. *As I was saying*, the miners themselves, the ones who dig through the red clay and such with shovels and their bare hands, they are hundreds of miles from the villages or cities they call home. Vermeulen Corp. supplies them with tents—and I'm not talking about North Face or Columbia Sportswear here. I mean ridge tents, tarps thrown over rope fastened to a pole on each end."

Whatever the opposite of "sagely" is, that's the way I nodded. It was always a humbling experience in the Boss's office. Not humiliating—I wasn't scolded as a schoolboy not knowing his lesson—but humbling. Out in the field, I always have everything completely under control down to the last detail. Even if the mission creeps into something else based on changing circumstances (poachers with cold feet, late-arriving cavalry, my local partner turning on me in the face of his hunter countrymen), I always have a Plan B, C, and D. For the record, I have never had to use a Plan D.

"Are you listening, H————?" he asked, uncannily able to detect my level of distraction.

"Yes, sir. Sorry. So these workers are put up in tent cities next to the mine, which are next to the river?"

He nodded now, apparently satisfied at my renewed attention. "These are the people of the Kasai basin who were raised on tales of the Kasai Rex as a way of keeping them from lingering near the river. Even without a ginormous man-eating cryptid running around, Congolese parents have good reason for their children to avoid the banks of the Kasai and the Congo River itself:

crocodiles, of course, but also snakes, poisonous lizards, and hippopotami, the last of which kills more people annually than all other predators combined ..."

I knew all of this, of course, but there was no way I was interrupting the Boss again. He went on for a bit about how slavers—and you bet your ass they are alive and well in Africa between the southern edge of the Sahara to the northernmost city of South Africa—also stalked the shores in boats, ready to leap into the water near the edge and grab a young boy or girl for a lifetime working in chains. When it sounded like he was done with his info dump, I asked, "So how many poachers do I need to recruit for this one?"

"Actually, not a one. We are much more concerned about the safety of the diamond miners and want to prevent them from killing what could be a slender-snouted crocodile. Their entire tent city has been leveled several times by what is reported to be a *very* large amphibious lizard."

"Slender-snouted crocs aren't very big, sir."

"No, but the Kasai Rex was humongous. Man-eating crocodile size." He took a long drag on his cigarette while he waited for me to understand what he was getting at.

I took a stab: "So it could be one of the region's big crocs—or a wandering saltwater croc, protected in Australia but not in Africa?"

"Bingo, old sport."

"Thank you, Mr. Gatsby," I said with a smile that he shared. "So that's why we don't need poachers, since they wouldn't be breaking any laws in the Congo, so we can't have them prosecuted."

"Again, right on the money."

I thought for a moment and then said, "If they're not endangered, why is The Organization involved? That's a bit out of our wheelhouse, isn't it?"

"Technically, you're correct. But two things: One, something is eating the impoverished Vermeulen mine workers on the Kasai, so *they* will be considered our endangered species. And number two ..."

I waited a few seconds, allowing him his dramatic pause. "And number two … ?"

The Boss shuffled some papers on his desk, not looking directly at me. Finally, he gathered his courage (*What the hell could this be?* I thought) and said, as matter-of-factly as imaginable, "I believe it might actually be Kasai Rex."

You could have knocked me over with a Velociraptor feather.

"The Congo's the deepest river in the world. Because of all the internal conflict there and the general lack of welcome for the White man after King Leopold and his enslavement of almost everyone in the Belgian Congo to cultivate the rubber-tree, most of the life in that river and its tributaries has never been catalogued. Kasai Rex was amphibious, and certainly large and vicious enough to eat a dozen people while destroying a tent city placed too near its territory."

"Sir, I would never contradict you—"

"Of course not."

"— but isn't a surviving dinosaur rather … unlikely?"

"It is," he said, lighting another cigarette with the end of his dying one, "and that would make it very endangered indeed, would it not?"

I could do nothing but nod.

"Besides, since we have you—our most effective and valuable operative—The Organization has a solemn obligation to protect the poor bastards working in the diamond mines from whatever this creature may be. Cryptid, living fossil, rare and endangered crocodile, common croc, or anything else. There have been hundreds of deaths at this one mine, but employment of any kind is so rare that new workers are hired immediately to keep the Vermeulen operation going."

I heard everything he said, but my mind stayed stuck on "most effective and valuable operative." That meant there were others. I reeled at the revelation.

"That said, it is becoming tougher for even Vermeulen to attract new workers with a supposed Kasai Rex killing dozens of people. The company is secretive as hell about its operations in Congo, but they do allow journalists in from time to time to show how they are providing for the poor Congolese with these jobs. We're going to send you in undercover as part of a documentary team, allowing you fairly free access to the camp and the river. Vermeulen knows every member of the *Cryptids Alive!* program will be armed for self-defense—against humans as much as any animal predators. It's a perfect opportunity for us to save the people, save and relocate the animal, and do it without fear of some whack-job poachers."

I had a question, but I couldn't just blurt it out. I had let my cheroot go out, so to buy time I slowly removed a match from my back pocket and struck it against my own forehead for entertainment, then made an elaborate show of relighting the cigar. I puffed a few times to get it going again before I asked, "Excuse my boldness, sir, but what the hell is *Cryptids Alive?*"

"It's a huge hit on the History Channel. They have ancient aliens building the pyramids, Bigfoot, supposed cover-ups at Area 51, ghost hunting, the truth about 9/11, all sorts of programming that is technically considered 'history' because its subjects happened in the past." He laughed. "Like anything one could research *hasn't* happened in the past. But *Cryptids Alive!* goes into areas of folklore and religion, trying to suss out the 'true story' of the mystery monster in question."

"So my face will be on camera? Haven't we spent millions to keep my identity a secret?"

"No, silly boy. Your cover is you're a boom-mike operator, a nobody with the production. And the History Channel is allowing The Organization (in one of its front incarnations, of course) complete access to the show before it is aired. By agreement, we can have deleted any footage even showing the back of your head as you fall into the river and are eaten by piranhas."

"Great, thanks."

The Boss glanced at the clock on the wall, one whose hands were the bones of a human pinky and forefinger. "This has been fun, H————. Your bags have already been packed for you, your go-to weapons included, so please go now and meet your *Cryptids Alive!* contact on top of our building. Their helicopter will take you all to the airport. As usual, you'll find your passage has already been booked and your security clearance set high enough to let you all zip right through security. Now go. Save something. Catch somebody evil. You know the drill."

That was the Boss's customary valediction, and I immediately left the comfort of that human-leather chair and left his office. Giving his secretary a nod as I walked to a different elevator, this one going only from the Boss's office to the helipad on the roof. I didn't get knocked out by nerve gas, so as soon as the doors opened and I saw the slim redhead leaning against a slick-looking corporate helicopter, my next adventure had begun.

# CHAPTER 4

"Ellie White," she said with a businesslike smile and her hand extended, which I shook, "*Cryptids Alive!* Glad to have you as part of the team, Doctor Russell."

*Doctor?* My new friend was shockingly attractive, her pale skin contrasting with her flaming hair, and her clipped Yankee syllables gave her a kind of "Lois Lane by way of Vassar" vibe. Since I didn't know what, if any, part of my cover story she had been informed of, so I said, "Glad to be your ... boom-mike operator?"

"If that's what it takes to get near the Kasai Rex, then you can call yourself the producer if you like!" she said with a laugh, then shook her head. "Actually, no—*assistant* producer. If soundman isn't good enough, you could be that. *I'm* the producer."

I wanted to give her one of those drawn out "Ohhhhh-KAYYYY..." responses, letting the crazy person know you were not going to contradict them directly but that you thought they were nuttier than squirrel shit. However, there was no reason to be a jerk right off the bat, so I said, "'Soundman' is fine. So I take it you know what I'm here for?"

She looked at me with very slightly narrowed eyes. "You're Brett Russell."

Now I narrowed my eyes slightly, a little more than hers but still pretty slightly. "That is correct."

"The Harvard cryptozoologist? We didn't even know Harvard *had* one until History sent us a couple of your papers in those journals. We followed up with the university and they confirmed that they do have a program but could say nothing more about it. I understand that the crypto community has to stay secret sometimes, but experiential journals distributed *only* to academics with nondisclosure agreements? *That* is impressive, Doctor Russell."

*What the heck was an 'experiential journal'?* "We, uh, we can't have the media making a field day out of a real and important academic discipline," I said, and I could see now what had happened: The Organization, which had its fingers in just about every pie ever baked, had worked out an understanding with the venerable institution to ... well, *lie* to the *Cryptids Alive!* people, maybe even the folks at History, maybe to its owners at A&E, maybe even to *its* owners, the big bosses at Hearst and Disney. From anything I had ever been able to tell, The Organization had, for all practical purposes, infinitely deep pockets from which it could have conjured anything from equipment to political lobbying to just a shit-ton of money. I don't know where it *got* all of that money—correction: *any* of that money—but they knew how to use it to get and do whatever it was they needed gotten or done.

Ellie gave a smile and a thumbs up to that and said, "We're on a tight schedule, Doctor—let me have your bag and you hop in the back there and get your ears on." She loaded my large duffel into the chopper and took her shotgun seat. All systems were go and we lifted off for Denver International with stops in Washington DC, Brussels, and Cameroon. In total, a 26-hour trip. Plenty of time to read on my iPad the papers I had supposedly written, which the Boss had gotten to me just in time for me to cram while we were in the air.

In the dossier the Boss had gotten to me just in time for me not to completely embarrass myself *and* blow my cover, I learned that Doctor Brett Russell was an academic with degrees from Yale and other Ivy League schools in folklore, zoology, and "Third World studies," whatever that was. According to the dossier, I had published multiple first-person accounts of cryptid "research" that I wouldn't think would ever make any academic journal anywhere—but apparently were perfect for the "experiential journals" listed, such as *Current Experiences in Cryptozoology*, *First-Person Academic Cryptid Encounters*, and *Quarterly of the Observed but Impossible*.

The articles themselves were written (by whom? How long had this been in the works? Was I really such a great operative that The Organization waited for me to become available before addressing the endangered croc or whatever it was down in the Congo?) more in the style of Nellie Bly documenting her trip around the world than that of a staid professor publishing his research: "Chupacabra Chase In Chihuahua"; "Hunting Hybrids in Hyderabad"; "Mole Valley Moose-Pig: Serious Signs or Surrey Swill?"

"It really is a pleasure to meet you, Doctor Russell," Ellie said once we had taken our first-class seats, and *oh my God* I would be ruined for coach forever. I felt a little bad for the rest of the crew back there, but not bad enough to change seats, especially since sitting here meant also being breathlessly complimented by a beautiful young woman. "Your narrative about nearly finding the Amomongo in the Philippines really made an impression on me! And then the close call with the Maryland Goatman—my goodness, Doctor R—"

"Brett, just Brett," I said with a smile, and she returned it with her million-watt teeth making the same contrast with her red lipstick that her skin did with her hair.

"Sorry—Brett. But your near-miss with the Inkanyamba Lake Monster reminded me of my own experience almost catching a glimpse of the Lake Chonji Monster in China. I can hardly believe I've been producing and hosting *Cryptids Alive!* for five seasons and have never come across your name."

I thought quickly and said, "Mainstream science doesn't show much respect for Cryptozoologists, Miss White—"

"Ellie," she said, and put her hand on mine on the armrest. My blood pressure rose dramatically, among other things. "And that is so true! Some people even say our show shouldn't be on an 'educational' network."

"Um, *yes*, that's exactly what I'm talking about. You'd have to be very brave to host a show on quasi-mythological creatures, I would think."

She demurely smiled in a way that showed complete agreement with my insightful comment.

"So I stay mostly under the radar, sharing information only with other cryptozoologists concealed, like me, in folklore programs or other tangentially related discipline's department." I looked at her seriously and added, "That's why I can't have my face on your show, you understand. Harvard would have to disavow all knowledge of me. I'd become a cryptid myself!"

We laughed, and although I spend a great deal of time trying to get information from indigenous populations about whatever chimerical beasts they think are terrorizing them—while simultaneously using their biased observations to figure out what possibly endangered animal we're *really* dealing with—this had to be the weirdest conversation I'd ever had. Was she crazy? Did she think *I* was crazy? Were we bullshitting each other, or was she sincere? I guess it didn't matter, but I felt like I was talking about the time I almost saw a giant rabbit leaving eggs all over my yard or how I almost tricked midgets dressed in green into giving me a pot of gold.

As much as I liked being touched by Ellie, I got down to business so I could take advantage of the next 26 hours and formulate my plan: "Tell me about Kasai Rex."

Her eyes sparkled. She took her hand back and settled herself in the plush seat to get in a good "holding forth" position. We were already in the air, so I casually tapped a few times on my iPad to start the voice recorder. "Okay, this may be the one we finally get on camera. There have been *dozens* of survivors, all reporting the same thing—a monster attacked their tent city, gobbling some people up *whole* and ripping others in half," she said with a glee that would have been unseemly if this weren't her entire *raison d'etre*. "They all described it the same, without any chance for assembling to make their stories match—they told the Vermeulen teams that came out each time to rebuild the tents and see to the workers' injuries. And, um, take away the parts of bodies that remained. Every one of them said it was a giant *Kasai Rex*, or at least as close as they could express it in the pidgin they use with the English- or Dutch-speaking Vermeulen men."

There's no need to make stories match when they've been told fairy tales since they were children to keep them from going by themselves the river, I thought, but said, "Their stories matched—so how did they describe the creature?"

"Well, *huge*, number one, and remember, the Congo River itself is largely unexplored—it's the deepest in the world, so there could be literally *anything* living there and we wouldn't know it."

That was a logical fallacy, but I let it slide. I was sure it would be far from the only one I would be hearing from the host and producer of a show about cryptids.

"And number two, they all said it was kind of red-colored—that's roughly the same color as the clay they dig in for diamonds, so obviously it must have gotten mud clinging to it when it came fully wet out of the river, since ancient reptiles were gray."

*Don't laugh. Do NOT laugh.* "What ..." I started, then had to swallow to keep a straight face, "... um, what makes you think the creature was an ancient reptile?"

"I guess I should have said ancient *amphibian,* much like a crocodile."

*VERY much like, I bet.* I did not say this out loud.

"So anyway, my thought about the mud was because such 'living fossils' are gray, and thus ancient surviving dinosaurs would be gray, whether land reptiles or amphibians. The survivors also said that the monster had a large hump on its back and moved like a lion. We've shot some talking head footage with a retired paleontologist who says there were actual dinosaurs who they think match those descriptions. He, quoted a report ... let me find it ..." She dug through her soft-leather briefcase and found the paper she was looking for. "Here we go:

> It was a large beast, at least 12 to 13 meters long. It was reddish in coloration, with brackish-colored stripes going down. The legs were thick; it reminded me of a lion, built for speed. It had a long snout and numerous teeth. It gorged itself on the rhinoceros, which twitched with life still in it. After the creature had eaten its fill, it returned to the jungle slowly, its belly full of flesh.

"The interview was *amazing,*" she continued. "It's like the paleontologist knew exactly what to say that would interest us and our viewers the most! He said that such a species could *easily* have survived deep in the Congo even though it supposedly had gone extinct."

"When?"

"About two weeks ago."

"No, I mean, when did these dinosaurs go extinct? Supposedly?"

"Oh!" she said with a self-deprecating chuckle. "Sorry—about 93 million years ago."

Hearing this educated, gorgeous woman talk like this was like watching a ballerina take a nose-dive into the orchestra pit.

"Doctor Russell? I mean, Brett? Still with us?"

"Just trying to formulate my next question to download all of the information you have for me. It's, um, fascinating." I took a goodly breath and said, "But what's to say what we're dealing with is some kind of dinosaur still stomping around almost 100 million years after its species died out?"

She gave a chuckle and, I swear, almost started her sentence with "DUH!" She said, "Because that's what a Kasai Rex *is*."

I could tell my eyes were wide and my nod slow, the way you agree with (a) a mathematician showing you an equation involving Greek letters; or (b) a crazy person who you're going to be sitting right next to all the way to Congo. (You may be able to guess which one was applicable.) "Oh, of course," I said, "it must be the alcohol affecting my cerebral cortex."

"Alcohol? But you haven't had anything to drink."

"Good point," I said, and signaled the First Class always-ready flight attendant: "Two whiskey sours, please. And whatever the lady would like."

# CHAPTER 5

At each stop on our way to Congo, we transferred to an airline with a lower safety rating until I thought about how long it would take to die in the utterly impenetrable African rainforest with two broken femurs. The answer to this, I think, would be both "not very long" and "far, far too long."

However, against all odds, we did make it to Tshikapa Airport, which was not technically what I like to call "paved." That was expected, however, since the airplane we took to the dirt landing strip on the Kasai tributary of the Congo River would have given Buddy Holly pause.

Ellie, her cameraman and her boom operator (yours truly) unfolded ourselves from the prop plane and sought out the nearest shade, a little bar with condensation on its bottles from the intense humidity of the steamy forest and river we had arrived in. The *Cryptids Alive!* actual sound man was to arrive along with all their equipment within the hour, since a single plane of the size servicing Tshikapa couldn't hold five people and the video equipment at the same time. (Or more people than it had seats, which was four. And two of those on the second plane would be piled with very carefully balanced video and audio equipment.)

Fortunately for us, while the Congolese speak a total of 242 distinct languages, the country's history as a Belgian colony meant that just about everyone spoke French. Ellie was fluent in French (I was still guessing Vassar) and I was competent. Her thirty-something cameraman, Gregory, who looked like he had been carved out of marble, muscles and all, had a smattering of French, as did the new cameraman we were waiting for, a kid named "Atari" by, I'm assuming, parents who were either stoned or assholes. Maybe both.

"Why'd you guys needs a replacement cameraman?"

"Ugh," Ellie groaned, and Gregory shook his head sadly. "We are right about to go after the Rocky Mountain Werewolf when our long-term camera guy, Bennie, gets *murdered* by a mugger who doesn't take Bennie's wallet but runs off with all his camera equipment."

"Yikes. Dangerous work," I said, but didn't add *creeping around for bullshit.*

"And this was our first night in your stomping grounds, in Denver. Atari had just put in for a camera position with History, specifying his preference to work on *Cryptids Alive!* I guess since this happened through no fault of any of us, I can hope that maybe this Atari can come up with some fresher shots than Bennie. His were getting kind of stale after five seasons."

We each had a tin mug of *pombe*, the local beer of Tshikapa. It would have been utterly vile to anyone who hadn't visited villages in Africa and Asia, but the three of us found it pretty tasty. And although I have no doubt we got the "white man's price," the beer was still cheap as hell.

The sun was already hot through the trees, even though it was only the middle of the morning. The humid air seemed to shimmer like the moisture was liquid in a pot over a fire.

Gregory was a sharp thirty-something who looked like he had gotten through film school only to find that employment was even better than being a starving *auteur.* He asked, "So, Mister Russell, why do you need a cover to come check out the Kasai Rex? I got the sound covered—we don't even *use* a boom mic—so there must be a reason."

"Call him Brett," Ellie said. "No one here needs to know he's a somebody."

"'Kay, sure, but how about it, Brett?"

Ellie knew my whole cover story, but the others would get just what they needed to know. "There could be something unprecedented here," I said to the sound man, "something that might need protection from people wanting to kill it."

"Hell, I don't care if they kill it, as long as we can get our camera and mics on it first. I don't want it to be like with the Yeti, where it must've been there like *just ten minutes* before we found its footsteps in the snow. They led to a crack in the side of the mountain where a Yeti could morph his body to fit, but humans with camera equipment couldn't. We got to make sure we don't scare it off like that. So I hear you on not letting the villagers or whatever attack it."

It sounded to me like the *creature* was doing most of the attacking, but I stayed silent. I had been in undercover situations before, although it had never been with a troupe of True Believers. "Let's just get a lay of the land before we decide how to proceed."

"*We?*" Ellie said with a crooked smile. "You weren't just using *Cryptids Alive!* to get you into the area unnoticed? You're staying with us?"

"That depends. Where are you staying, exactly?" I responded with a smirk of my own.

"As close to the action as possible. If the Kasai Rex is trampling villagers and eating people alive, I want our camera set up to roll at any kind of movement and the crew and myself close enough to wake up at any commotion."

I looked at Gregory with an *Is she for real?* expression, and he nodded at me with a knowing smile. "Our Miss White is as hardcore as they get, man. It's kind of inspiring."

"Oh, lord, Greg, stop. We'll be staying in tents, just like the miners. If the thing attacks in the night, we'll have our sodium lamps ready to light up the whole camp." She saw the look on my face and quickly added, "Don't worry—we'll be on the *other* edge of the tent city, the one opposite the river where there's a little swell. That way, if the Kasai Rex attacks, we'll not only have the best vantage point to capture the action, we'll also be relatively safe."

*Relatively.* I definitely noted the word as I heard, then saw, the beater aircraft no doubt carrying Atari and the equipment wobbling in toward a landing on the Tshikapa "runway."

"Time to see what a *Ghost Chasers* cameraman looks like," Gregory said.

Ellie turned to the bartender and asked in French, "How do we get to the Vermeulen diamond mine from here?"

"*Voyage du sud-east,*" the barman said, pointing down the wide Kasai, which we could only just see from our stools. "*Vous aurez besoin d'un véhicule, est-ce pas?*"

I lifted my eyebrows at Ellie in languid surprise. "You didn't hire a car? A Hummer, whatever they use here to lug equipment in 104 degrees and 98 percent humidity?"

She stammered a bit: "I was—I was told the Vermeulen people would be picking us up for the short drive—"

"*Moan amies!*" came a jocular voice from the direction of the runway. This must have been Atari, a chubby Black kid, as he and the pilot dragged dollies loaded with production equipment. When they reached the bar, Atari handed the pilot a five-dollar bill like he was a porter, and the pilot seemed happier than a porter ever would have at the tip, shaking all of our hands before heading back to his plane to take a nap, it looked like.

Gregory put out his big paw. "So you're Atari, huh? Surprised you made it with, y'know, this extra ballast," the incredibly fit man said to Atari, poking him gently with a forefinger.

"Hell, you weigh more than me, man!" Atari said with a laugh. "And at least if my weight brought the plane down, I could *bounce!*"

*Shit!* Quite the introduction! Oh, I liked this kid already.

Ellie shook Atari's hand and introduced herself and me. When the new cameraman ordered himself a sickly-sweet African Coke, Ellie leaned over to me and said, "Camera guys and sound guys tease each other mercilessly, like two kittens making sure they're both into fun. They play *rough*." We both laughed.

"Here comes the cavalry," Gregory said, and we all looked to see a beat-up station wagon manufactured, if I had to guess, in the first half of the 1980s. But it had "Vermeulen" stenciled on its side and looked like it would have plenty of room for all of us and our equipment. Also on its side were more than a dozen bullet holes. That was interesting. Behind the wheel was a smiling man with skin so dark his face was almost hard to make out in the Congolese sun.

"TV people, yes?" he said in English. "You come to see Kasai monster, yes?"

"That's us," Ellie said in French—no sense in making the poor driver struggle to understand—and her two crewmen loaded up the back of the station wagon. "You'll take us to the mine, where the workers live?"

"Yes, pretty lady," the driver said, apparently still taking advantage of this opportunity to practice his English, "I take you people all there, yes?"

"Yes, please," she said in English and gave the driver a smile that I could tell made him fall in love immediately, "take us there."

\*\*\*

Before we could go very far, however—just out of sight of the little bar—a military-surplus–looking open-air Jeep cut right in front of us, four men in green camo and green berets loaded inside. There was also a *goddamn machine gun* mounted above the windshield. Seeing the belligerent attitude of the men as each hopped out of the Jeep and approached Bonte's vehicle, the bullet holes in the station wagon's side suddenly made a lot of sense.

Bonte immediately opened his door and got out to face the men, which to me—and I admit that after a little more than an hour in Congo I wasn't an expert on domestic relations—seemed like a very bad idea. So I got out as well, Ellie making a move to grab my arm, but I thought that the militia members (there were no official markings on the Jeep, so I assumed these weren't actual Army soldiers) would be much less likely to shoot a white foreigner than a fellow Congolese national.

The head of the group—I guessed this by his place in the Jeep's passenger seat and also that he was the one at the front, spewing rapid words in a language I couldn't even place. Swahili? Kikongo? I didn't take it as a good sign, because the people of the disjointed country calling itself Congo most often spoke French in order to smooth communications.

This captain of the Jeep didn't want things smooth. To me that indicated nationalism. Being in an armed Jeep with pseudo-uniforms said to me "militant nationalism." That's the kind that gets you dead a lot.

Captain Jeep was rapidly firing words at Bonte, approaching him in a beeline with his face thrust forward. Our driver, for his part, seemed calm and he answered back in what sounded to me like that same language. His answers did nothing to ease the fire in Captain's eyes, and the belligerent man looked outraged that a white man was out of the vehicle and approaching him as well.

"What's he saying, Bonte?" I asked under my breath in English, hoping the militia members didn't know the language well enough to catch the words of my aside.

"Ah, the usual," our driver said, his nonchalance bordering on somnambulism, "like telling me I am a slave for working for Vermeulen. Threatening to end my life right here, that kind of talk, you know?"

I did, indeed. "Tell him we are not mine executives—we are a television crew here to document worker abuse." Maybe they were Marxists and would like that particular bite of cheese.

The bulging eyes of Captain Jeep took me in and his men peered into the back of the station wagon and made some kind of report to him as they returned to his side.

"What now?" I asked Bonte through a mostly closed mouth.

"They say there don't seem to be weapons, just cameras and that kind of thing," he said quietly to me.

"I have a semiautomatic pistol tucked into the back of my pants."

"My Uzi is under the front seat."

So much for no weapons, but the four hungry-looking men had us at a particular advantage: they outnumbered the two of us, for one thing, and for another, their weapons were already in their hands.

Bonte spoke a long sentence to the Captain, during which no one moved.

At the end of the speech, Captain Jeep's black face broke into a yellow smile and he babbled something that sounded like it was funny to him and his men—they all smiled, too—but perhaps would not as funny to the rest of us. He pointed inside the car, and the sickly grinning henchmen yanked one of the back doors opened and hauled out Atari, whose eyes were wide with fear. Captain Jeep gave him a smile and a "Wassup?" nod, then said something to him in the African language none of us understood. Then they stood him right next to Bonte, which was very not good.

I yelled at the Captain, "Release that man now. You know what *now* means, asshole? *NOW*." Then I added as quietly as possible to Bonte, "What the hell did you say to them?"

Bonte said, "I told him they would be hunted down if they killed a white man visiting Vermeulen."

"Aw, Jesus."

"So they say they kill your black man."

"What was that the boss said to Atari?"

"There are a lot of, what do you call, dialects in Congo. I have no idea what he said."

"But he thinks the *American* would? Why, because he's black?"

"Mister Russell, my good new friend, I have no idea. But he will kill me and also him."

"Yeah, I get it. But don't worry. I think we—"

The operatic anger of Ellie White's voice slashed through everyone's conversation. "*Parlez-vous français, connard?!*" she screamed as she got out of the station wagon and came around to yell in Captain Jeep's bemused face. Douglas also got out, I'm sure damned if he was going to stay in the car in a crisis. "*Eh? Eh? PARLEZ, PUTAIN!*"

"*Nous ne parlons français,*" Cappy said with his chin jutting out in defiance of the raging American woman. "*Nous sommes congolaise.*"

I didn't need an interpreter for that. *We don't speak French. We are Congolese.* In French. It was, how do you say, *très ironique, non*?

Ellie ignored his proud statement and continued to let him have it in French whether he wanted it or not. (I'm thinking "not.") "*Si vous touchez un cheveu sur la tête de ce garçon, je vais retirer vos testicules et les forcer dans votre anus!*"

It was too fast and had too many words in it for me to follow, although I did catch "*testicules*" and "*anus.*" I looked at Bonte, who said a bit shyly, "She say, um, she prefers it if your companion is not harmed."

Captain Jeep's smile turned a little, turning into a sneer. I could also not help but notice that the three "soldiers" had unholstered their pistols, not seeming sure whether to point them at Atari or at Ellie. She hocked a loogie roughly the size of a quarter and launched it into the Captain's ugly face.

Now all the henchmen's guns were pointed at Ellie.

I yelled, "Hey! Boss man! How about English? Do you understand English?"

The scowling captain designed to look at me. "A slight little."

That was perfect. I needed to tell Gregory to cause a distraction, but that might have been just within the militia mens' grasp of English. So I thought for a second of the most idiomatic phrase I could to get my meaning across, and belted out to the big sound man standing fifteen feet away: "It's all-eyes-on-Greg ShowTime! Gregor, do me a solid and shit in their Corn Flakes."

A grin appeared on Gregory's face and he … well, he then made a sound like a gibbon being sexually violated, jumped up in the air and started skipping in a direction that went slightly behind the four men. None of them could help it (in all fairness, I wouldn't have been able to, either), but they all turned their heads to watch the sudden madness of the big American.

It was perfect. Ellie moved with incredible precision—especially considering she didn't know the plan, and it wasn't much of a plan anyway—and shoved her hand forward and under Cappy's scrotum and squeezed one of his balls so hard it almost made *me* throw up. He went down like a sack of rivets, squealing like a pig that suddenly stopped screaming because it was projectile-vomiting.

"Ellie, get down!" I shouted, the heads of the three henchmen already coming back around in confusion, their weapons still in their hands.

I swept my pistol out from behind me and *Pop! Pop! Pop!* I dropped all three sons of bitches by creating huge holes in their chests, right where vital organs like to live. Ellie, Atari, and even Gregory—who stopped skipping when the shots rang out—stared at what I had just done, and then at me, mouths open, eyes super-wide.

*"What the shit, man? What'd you do that for?"* Atari shouted in real anger.

That literally stopped me in mid-run. "How can you even ask that? They were about to *murder* you."

"I'm Buddhist, man," he said, looking at the bodies. "We don't condone killing."

"Condone—you—*what?* Just grab their guns and let's get out of here," I commanded Atari and Ellie. The Dalai Lama there snapped out of it and swiftly collected the semiautomatics from the dead men while the show's elegant host kicked the slowly raising gun out of Captain Jeep's hand, then brutally kicked him in his already mangled balls, making him forget all about anything else in the universe except his agony. She calmly picked up his gun, flipped on the safety, and stuffed it into her pocket.

I was impressed and I said so as we moved to get back into the car, adding, "Why didn't you *shoot* him?"

"I'm not a murderer," she said. "You *had* to kill those men to keep them from killing us. Thank you, by the way. The Little General no longer posed a threat."

I sighed and let my chin drop. "Great, one of the world's most dangerous countries, and I've got a group full of conscientious objectors."

"I don't give a shit," Gregory said. "I'm sorry I didn't get to shoot those assholes myself."

We all laughed, but one voice was missing. Atari said, "Hey, where did Bonte go—"

*RAT-TAT-TAT-TAT-TAT-TAT!*

*KA-BOOOOOOOM!* The air shoved past us, hot as blazes, then swept back the other way.

The four of us ducked down, but we could easily see through the non-existent windows of the Vermeulen station wagon that Bonte must have jumped back and grabbed his under-the-seat Uzi the second the Captain went down. Since I had taken point on putting down the three stooges, Bonte took his machine gun to the Jeep and filled it full of very hot lead, including the gas tank.

The Jeep jumped three feet in the air—Bonte ran away as fast as he could to help not get ripped apart by shrapnel—and fell in a crumpled heap that filled the air with its column of thick black smoke.

We were all sitting in the vehicle by the time he got back from hauling ass in the other direction and swung open the driver-side door and got in. He was out of breath and sweating, but his grin was something to behold. None of us knew what to say, so we just smiled back at him.

Finally he closed his door and started the engine. "I like this job. I don't like these guys," he said in French, and got us back on the road. "They try to scare Vermeulen Mining away so they can have all the diamonds. But people think Vermeulen treat people bad? These 'soldiers' would make slaves out of every miner. Even when you don't have much to eat, even when you have to risk Kasai Rex to provide for your family ..."

We all sat rapt, listening.

"... even then, you remember when the Belgians didn't just own a company. You remember the days of rubber trees, when they owned your people. Freedom is everything."

# CHAPTER 6

We sat in relative silence the rest of the way, but in pretty good cheer for having thwarted whoever those people were from whatever it is they had wanted to do.

It was only a few miles from the airport to the Vermeulen Mining Corp.'s tract near the edge of the river, but it was a bumpy, hot, and uncomfortable few miles. Bonte apologized for not having working air-conditioning in the station wagon, and suggested that we passengers press our faces against the windows, all of which (including the front windshield) lost their glass long ago and now were crisscrossed by metal bars on the outside. He said he would drive faster to provide us with a breeze.

"Do people try to steal diamonds out of your car?" Atari asked, checking out the window cages. Ellie started to translate but Bonte bravely held up his hand to indicate he would try to answer in English.

"No, this car not diamond car. *That* diamond car." He pointed at an ancient—but sturdy-looking—armored car parked right at the entrance to the mining camp. "This car ..." he said, struggling to find the right words, then switched to French for Ellie to translate: "This car has radio, so I put extra security on it."

Gregory looked around at the thick forest and wide river surrounding us. "Tshikapa has a radio station?"

Bonte smiled and said, "*Nous avons la Voix de l'Amérique pour l'Afrique,*" which even Atari could understand, and then "*Et de nombreux programmes chrétiens,*" which Ellie translated as "And a whole bunch of Christian programs."

"Oy vey," Gregory mumbled.

"But it does not matter what stations of radio we have," Bonte said, still smiling. "I do not listen anyway."

"No?"

"The radio is broken."

I put my head down, unable to suppress my amusement. *Welcome to Africa.*

Passing the armored car, we could see the tent city, comprised of what must have been a hundred A-shaped ridge tents, some with cooking smoke wafting out. We would be staying in a tent as well, but one of more comfortable—and modern—design, built to shelter four people (and which we had brought with us). Again, ours would be on a small rise overlooking the tent city, which stood between us and the river. Any crocodile attack—or magical lizard attack—would be caught on video, and my bags contained the croc-capturing materials I needed. Looking at the muscles on Gregory and Bonte as well as the weight on Atari, I saw that I had the brute force needed (maybe with a few grateful miners helping out) to snag the croc, tie off its snout, and turn the one-ton animal onto its back so it could be tranquilized. So I was confident I could, with the help of my fellows, secure for transport what I had decided was most likely a *Crocodylus porosus*, a saltwater crocodile that had lost its way and ended up trying to navigate the tributaries of the Congo River. The things were *huge* and they were *fast*. I could totally see a population fed stories about the Kasai Rex since childhood "seeing" the cryptid, since the real thing was probably just as fierce.

However, I lacked one very important arrow in my quiver in my potential pursuit of the saltwater man-eater: the species was anything but endangered, officially labeled as one of "least concern" by the scientists watching over the animals of the world.

If it really were *C. porosus*, my mission here would technically be over and I'd technically have to extract myself back to the States immediately, my set of skills no doubt being demanded by another Organization priority. Same thing with my second guess at the identity of this monster, which was the most dangerous indigenous African amphibian, the Nile crocodile, the largest apex predator in the world after its saltwater-dwelling cousin. It, too, was thriving and thus considered an animal of "least concern" in terms of extinction risk.

*Least concern.* Words that I simultaneously loved—*Hey! An animal not being destroyed by man!*—and loathed, since there was nothing I was technically allowed to do to save the creature from being killed (and probably eaten by the starving miners) and even less I could to protect the miners without the imprimatur of The

Organization exerting upon the mining company the moral pressure to move their people out of harm's way, which they wouldn't do with a non-endangered animal. The Organization also wouldn't arrange an airlift for a non-endangered animal living in its natural habitat (in this case, the rivers of the Eastern Hemisphere). And if I lied in order to get a chopper team out here—or, more likely, a good-sized pickup truck—then I'd be in hot water with my employer, something I'd really rather avoid.

If the supposed Kasai Rex turned out to actually be a member of an endangered population, however, then I could save it *and* the villagers whose mine had encroached upon the unidentified mystery animal's territory.

Before I even worried about any of that, I needed—and I assume Ellie needed as well—to talk to Daan Vermeulen, the head of the diamond-mining company he had inherited from his father, who had inherited it from his. These Dutch-owned companies operating in Africa kept their cards held very close to their chests. The bare fact that they were allowing a television crew to video the mines and conditions as a part of *Cryptids Alive!* seeking the killer cryptid was astounding.

Vermeulen must have had quite an interest in resolving the situation, considering how much mining companies were reviled all over the world for exploiting the poor bastards who had to roast animal skins to eat while they dug up millions of dollars worth of rocks for their corporate slave masters. Congo's diamonds were no longer what they called "conflict" or "blood" diamonds, since there was no Sierra Leone–like civil war using the miners as pawns to move and kill at their pleasure. (Not that it kept wholesalers, retailers, and end customers from snapping up even the bloodiest of blood diamonds.)

But what there was, obviously, was a violent militia presence that wanted the riches contained in the Kasai river mud. Clever and amazing as our quartet was, we had undoubtedly gotten lucky that the Captain and his Tennilles weren't expecting guests of Vermeulen Mining to be carrying weapons. I can't imagine that would happen again, but I also couldn't imagine that the militia would be allowed to enter the camp at will. I didn't see any police presence in Tshikapa, which didn't surprise me considering we had gone straight from the airport to the mines. We did have to pass through a security gate, however, with two heavily armed guards, one packing an AK-47 and the other a longer-range rifle. They would be able to see anyone coming since the road a mile into the mine area was very straight, and could probably take out anyone threatening before they got close enough even to set off a car bomb or throw a grenade. These guards waved Bonte and his vehicle full of us Americans through without stopping us. My hands were shaking a little, the adrenaline slow to leave my system. (I had killed men before, every time like this one under the threat of imminent violent death, but never three in one go. I could see Ellie's hands shake, too, from her judicious application of her ninja five-point palm exploding scrotum technique.

I had to shake the violence from my mind if I were to fit in with this crew, but well-justified or not, my killing three men would haunt me just as my self-defense murders of the past always have. I took a deep breath and returned my focus to killer zoological oddities that hated diamond miners, apparently.

The whole situation was beyond weird, but I was with cryptid hunters (ahem) and I myself was an actual cryptid hunter in my way, so I guess "weird" was going to be our *modus operandus*. There were things going on here that had nothing to do with endangered animals *or* magical time-travel cryptids. Or mining. What exactly *was* going on here?

None of this was technically my concern, but I had to admit I was curious as hell about those questions and the bigger one, the elephant in the room: *Why was Vermeulen allowing us here? Forget about* allowing *us—hell, they* invited *us*.

Bonte whisked us to the front of a squat, bunker-like concrete building without signage and with windows so small looking out upon the river that it reminded me of a Mafia boss's safe house. It was the size of a small-town Wal-Mart, one-story and wide. One entrance I could see, mud encrusted against the doors.

Bonte got out too, and shook each of our hands between taking our equipment out of the back of the station wagon. "Our friendship is sealed in blood now, my Americans. I will die for you if necessary. Just call upon Bonte and I will come."

As our newly sealed-in-blood friend got in the car and waved goodbye, I took a closer look at the mud spatters and streaks on the bunker entrance. Some of them looked to be about shoulder-high and grouped and smeared like fists had been beating on the door. Pissed-off miner looking for a little respect? Or scared-for-his-life miner seeking shelter during an attack? There didn't seem to be any blood on the door, which was reassuring in the smallest and mildest way possible.

Ellie made to press the intercom button next to the door, but before she could the door opened and a tall, gaunt figure stood in the doorway. He had slightly longish gray hair, a gray moustache and goatee, and a gray suit that probably cost more than the airplanes we arrived in. "The television crew," he said and extended a long hand to Ellie, which she shook with a smile. "Vermeulen Mining is delighted to welcome you. I'm Daan Vermeulen, and yes, I'm one of the owners ... along with my brothers and sisters, my fellow heirs back in Antwerp."

We all smiled along with his slight self-deprecation.

"So do come in! And wipe your feet first, won't you? Living here has produced in me a strong aversion to ... *mud*."

He spat that last word in a way I could completely relate to. I also enjoyed his accent—Dutch, plainly, but his English was absolutely perfect. Better than mine, probably. We each shook his bony hand as we wiped our feet and entered the safe house. Or company building, whatever. Those fist smears had left an indelible mark upon my mind as much as on the door.

The building was strange as hell. To the right, visible through large windows were the usual trappings of a busy office: desks, cubicles, (white) men and women in business casual seated or hustling from one place to another, a line of mostly open dark-wood doors on the far end of the office for the important people. The ones that were shut sported security keypads next to them.

This office stretched all the way to the back of the building but took up just about a third of its width. On the other side of the hallway carpet runner, completely open except for the presence of support beams, was a huge and empty ... well, *cavern* is the only way I can really convey what it felt like. It was dark, muddy bare footprints commingled with muddy shoeprints, smears against the walls.

I could practically smell the fear, even panic, emanating from that side of the building. I could also see Ellie grin at her crew, no doubt feeling incredibly excited that a cryptid (of course) had caused this kind of fearful reaction inside a concrete bunker. This was what she had been waiting for. This was *real* at last.

At least that's what I thought her grin meant. Maybe she was just happy to be out of the mud, I don't know.

Daan Vermeulen stopped about midway through the building's depths and opened a door for us on the right. We stepped inside and through the office to his door. (We knew it was his because it had a bright and well-polished nameplate.) He entered a code on the keypad and opened that door for us as well.

The office was *nice*, which I expected, of course: the smell of well-oiled leather and wood, the desk *accoutrements* and even a small telescope all in brass, and the tasteful art and lighting arrangement made me feel like I had entered the Explorer's Club in London.

What really stuck, however, was that the interior dimensions of the room were obviously smaller than what one would expect given the spacing of the other offices along the wall and their apparent depth spied through their open doors.

Vermeulen's office was reinforced with another foot of concrete on all sides. It made the room even more cozy, but my mind was running with wild surmises. You didn't need feet of rebar and concrete to keep a saltwater crocodile—or hell, an elephant—from getting into your safe house office. So what was the boss being protected from in here? Angry workers and their families? Everyone had looked pretty sedate when Bonte drove us past the tent city. Maybe the diamonds were stored in this office once the company had paid pennies to the miners for each one. But, in that case, why not just have a reinforced vault? Surely Daan Vermeulen didn't need to keep one hand on his store of diamonds, Scrooge McDuck–style.

Or was it to protect him from ... cue the dramatic music ... a *KASAI REX?!?*

No, it was not.

Mythical creatures are called "mythical" for a reason. That reason is that *they do not exist.* We have video footage of wild mountain fuzzball cats that no one has actually seen for fifty years. Our satellites have dispelled the myths of Atlantis and alien messages written in flattened cornstalks. (The first is nowhere to be found and the last is too small to see even from very low orbit, hence useless for space navigation. Boom, *science.*)

What *do* exist are very hungry, angry, territorial predators that do not appreciate their areas being encroached upon by humans. The Organization has very effective ways, as you saw earlier, of locating these animals—which are, although fearsome, just regular old animals, no need for mystery lizards hidden in the admittedly vast and uncharted Congo jungle and river. And then we extract them so they won't endanger or be endangered by humans for a long time. Oh, and we try to take down as many poaching assclowns as we can at the same time.

But all *this?* Daan Vermeulen's office was essentially a man-vault. That huge space that looked like Woodstock after every attendee dropped bad acid, the lack of windows in the building ... something was going on here that I had no faculty to process. I like a situation where I can punch someone in the face, kick them in the balls or the gut, handcuff and neutralize them. Heck, *shoot* them (even if it is with a tranq dart, which I have done). And then I like to call in the good guys and get the poachers *and* our dangerous animals taken to places where they'd stay for years to come.

But ... again: *This?* I had nothing.

Anyway, Vermeulen bade us all to sit in the lovely chairs and sat behind his elegant desk. He steepled his fingers and said with a smile in his slightly Old World accent, "I know what all of you are thinking. Vermeulen Mining—just like DeBeers and all the other big diamond concerns—has been kicking film crews out for decades. We sue reporters and magazines, essentially for telling the truth but getting enough of some detail wrong that we can sue them for libel. And *win*, mind you. So—"

"Why let in a monster-hunting show?" Ellie interrupted. "Is it because you think we have no credibility, is that it? So anything we show in video or whatever has to be bullshit, since you think cryptids are bullshit? You want to use us to discredit any reports of abuse just by it being shown in the background of our search for the Kasai Rex."

Daan Vermeulen sat completely still, his fingers still pressed into an A. Then he looked at me and said, "Quite the spitfire, is she not?"

"She takes her job seriously, Mister Vermeulen. As we all do."

His eyebrows raised in surprise. "Well, then! A united front!" He cleared his throat, unsteepled his fingers, and leaned forward in his chair. "Actually, Miss White, I am also someone who takes his job very seriously. And my job is keeping miners digging in those holes out there and bringing me the diamonds hidden there."

Ellie leaned forward. "Is part of your job using Congolese militia bullies to keep your miners frightened and working?"

Atari and I looked at each other. Didn't see *this* conversation popping up.

He paused to fix his gray eyes on each of us: First Ellie, then me, then Atari, then Gregory. It was an effective thing to do if he meant to keep us listening closely.

"What do you think you know about these 'militias,' as you have decided to call them?"

Ellie said, "We just killed three of them on the way here and blew up their vehicle. I think I might have sterilized the leader of their little troupe by ripping off his testicles."

Vermeulen looked at her with wide eyes and a small smile grew as he gazed at Atari, Gregory, and then me. "This is true? You American cowboys have already starting shooting your guns?"

"Yep," I said, Gary Cooper–style.

"Ha! Well done! May I ask what the occasion was for this fireworks show?"

"They stopped us," Atari said. "They dragged me out of the car and were going to shoot me along with Bonte. Black-on-black violence, man, it's got to stop."

There was a ripple of amusement, and then Gregory spoke up: "We had to create a distraction so Mister Russell could shoot them down. They were going to kill us all. It seemed they wanted to send a message to your company."

Vermeulen nodded gravely, his smile gone. "So, Miss White, you see that we are not in league with the terrorists—which is what they are, *terrorists* trying to force Vermeulen Mining out of the country through acts of violence. On the contrary, we oppose them for our very existence here. They are not like real militia groups, wanting power through social unrest and ultimately a civil war. No, they want the riches of these mines for themselves."

"And you don't?" Ellie said.

"If we do not have miners, we do not have a business. Yes, I pay them very little for the rough stones they bring to us, and they don't get paid at all if they don't find anything to bring us in the first place. But that is the market here—diamonds are in great abundance, as are buyers, not only us but many local middlemen not associated with my company, and they pay even less than we do. It is simple supply and demand, Miss White."

"So why *are* we being allowed in?"

"As I say, I need these ni—" he started to say a very unsavory word indeed, then remembered Atari was sitting right there and altered his verbal course. "I need these *people* to dig in the mud, go down narrow fifty-foot-deep holes, spend their entire days searching for dusty rocks that they cannot feed to their families. I cannot have them fearing attack by a supernatural monster, especially not when something really *is* eating miners and stomping their living area flat in a rage."

"The Kasai Rex is not *supernatural*, Mister Ver—"

"No, of course not. But whatever is attacking my miners, I need them—and the world—to see that perhaps it is a giant crocodile, perhaps a group of them, perhaps a mass of gorillas swinging on vines who have decided vegetarianism is no longer for them. Perhaps a feral rodent of unusual size. Perhaps an army of them—Sumatran monkey-rats have been known to swarm over river areas when the water level rises, eating everything in sight. Maybe a man-eating anaconda. Whatever it is, it scares many miners from coming to work."

"And it's killed a lot of them, too," Gregory said.

"Yes, well, of course we are concerned about that as well. Dead men cannot dig for diamonds." He must have noticed the appalled expressions on our faces and added, "That, em, is our first concern, of course. But we need to show the people of Congo that there is no mysterious monster lurking here to eat them. Whatever it is, it's just animals, and animals can be killed."

I was sitting right next to Ellie, so I could see her eyes narrow and her jaw stiffen.

*Oh, shit.*

"So you wanted *Cryptids Alive!* to come here—you *paid* for us to come here—because you think we won't find any actual cryptids? That, totally the opposite—that we'll basically *prove* there is no Kasai Rex terrorizing the village here?"

Vermeulen cleared his throat like one does when about to say something you *know* the other party is not going to want to hear. "Miss White, when my company was developing the idea of bringing in 'experts' to calm these simple people's fears to stop the attrition of our miners, I was given DVDs of your program. You have made a career out of proving absolutely nothing."

Strangely, Ellie's head didn't explode at this comment. She just looked defiant. It was very sexy, indeed. (Am I a sexist pig? No. I would have felt the same way if a man was sitting there looking exactly like Ellie White. She *happened* to be incredibly attractive—but her defining feature was her *will*. And I like my women strong. And also women who are actually men who look like hot women.)

"I have gathered the ni—damn my eyes, all apologies. I have gathered the *people*, the miners, and told them that *Cryptids Alive!* was coming here to kill the Kasai Rex *or* prove that it doesn't exist. These people barely eat; they haven't seen your show. But they do believe in this monster. I'm sure you noticed the large space on the interior of this building, mud-streaked as if there had been hundreds of panicked diamond miners herded in there."

I was listening.

"It looks that way because there *were*. Something came out of the river and ate a few unfortunate men, but we got the rest of the miners inside here inside our protective building until the danger had ceased. They all said to a man that it was Kasai Rex, a giant four-legged dinosaur with jaws like a crocodile and a fin on its back—"

"Kasai Rex doesn't have a fin," Ellie interrupted.

"Kasai Rex doesn't *exist!*" Vermeulen barked, pounding his fist on the dark polished wood of his desk. "Excuse me. Look, to answer your question of why we are letting you in here, why we *asked* you to come, is to either show that this monster is real, in which case everyone in the world will come to try to hunt it down—or, and obviously I believe this is the case—that there is no such cryptic monster."

I could *feel* Ellie wanting to correct it to *cryptid*, but she stayed silent.

"Meaning that not only is Vermeulen Mining *not* putting people's lives in danger, we are actually *protecting* the miners by calling in 'experts' to examine whether there is unusual danger here, considering that it is Congo. This is a dangerous place. But it's not *supernaturally* dangerous—"

Ellie shook slightly, but held it together.

"—and miners need to come and work here if they are to survive at all. These so-called militia forces want to take over our diamond operation by forcing us out, killing our miners so no one will come to work here while Vermeulen mining is the business concern, but we protect them by allowing them to live in the tents on-site. Are we Habitat for Humanity, giving aid to the world's poorest darkies?" He shut his eyes, then opened them and said to Atari, "Please forgive my crudeness, an old habit among us former colonials. But no, we are not UNICEF, we are not Father Christmas, handing out goodies. We are a business in a ruthless and lethal area of the world. But we do what we can to protect our workers ... because we need them. And *Cryptids Alive!* is part of our retention effort. Okay?"

That was a lot to chew on, but Ellie finally answered, "Okay," and the rest of us gave quick nods to show that we were behind our leader.

"One final thing and then I shall let you go about your work. This is completely off the record and Vermeulen Mining will not hesitate to sue you out of existence if you repeat it."

"Jeez," Atari mumbled.

"We have *no* idea what is out there. Our company has been here since King Leopold in 1901, and none of our mines have ever experienced anything like this. Maybe it is a Kasai Rex. Maybe it is a magical angry unicorn. Whatever it is, we *want* you to identify it so we can kill it. So film anything you want, talk to the miners, talk to the villagers nearby, just *get rid of their fear.*" Vermeulen swallowed, his Adam's apple taking a single bob, and he looked suddenly like a man haunted by ghosts. "If you cannot tell, I am desperate. This is no longer a family business; we are traded on the Amsterdam Stock Exchange. That means we have a board of directors, and our losses from fewer and fewer miners are public record. The diamonds are there in plenty, but people are becoming very reluctant to dig for them when they think a Kasai Rex is going to come and gobble them up. My board wants to sell Vermeulen mining. I have worked my entire adult life and most of my childhood here in Congo, building this company."

"On the backs of the poor—" Ellie started, but was almost immediately cut off.

"I have said all I will say on that matter, Miss White. You have your access, you have a place to put your tent, and you all may eat with the office staff at the cafeteria inside this building. Now please go and *find out what the holy hell is going on out there.*"

# CHAPTER 7

Our first task was to set up the tent. The *Cryptids Alive!* team, including Ellie, worked like a Swiss watch at assembling their three-room tent that they used when just missing seeing cryptids, and I almost had to laugh at the expensive technological wonder of their huge tent on the swell of the hill, looking down on the slave city in their open-air tarps flung over two sticks and a line of rope. The TV crew didn't need me for this, so I stood and surveyed our temporary neighborhood.

"So we are *literally* looking down on the black miners," I said, taking in what I could see from the higher place, which was a lot: the tent city, the network of dug holes in the red clay of the riverbank, the green Kasai River itself, and thick jungle on the other side that looked practically impregnable.

"Oh, great, we're the plantation masters," Gregory said. "I feel like an asshole."

"Aw, dude, if this up here is the plantation, what does that make me? Uncle Tom the House Boy?" Atari said with a laugh that we all shared, us white folks a little gratefully, I think.

As I tried to get good bearings on where people did what they did here—we were pretty near the front entrance, and Bonte honked and waved when he drove by in that *Mad Max* station wagon—I noticed something about the jungle just opposite the mine, on the other side of the river. Especially in the noonday sun, the chaos of jungle was dark beneath the treetops, looking more foreboding than ever. But I did notice one thing: there was about a fifteen-foot "hole" in the mad foliage and the mud from that hole to the river was smoothed, as if something had been repeatedly dragged from the trees into the water.

Maybe it was a pair of crocodiles that attacked together, moving side by side into and out of the river after sating themselves on miner flesh. But crocs didn't really hunt or feed like that. There were plenty of other nasty candidates I'd be looking into tomorrow, both online with our satellite link and on foot in that exact path in the jungle. I planned to go by myself, but if *Cryptids Alive!* wanted to come with and get some footage, fine by me.

\*\*\*

We spent most of the afternoon checking the video and sound equipment, and I sent detailed reports of what I had been doing back to The Organization via the uplink. They were acknowledged by the Boss in his usual way, a terse email saying only "Understood. Keep us posted." I knew there had to be an "us," of course, or else The Organization wasn't an organization at all, and their influence and buying power across the globe would be impossible to explain. But I did wonder sometimes who "they" were paying me so handsomely to save endangered animals.

We ate dinner in the Vermeulen commissary, mostly to save the effort of hauling out the cooking stuff and sending delicious smells of cooking food wafting down into the tent city, where they were eating—like slaves everywhere, official or not—pieces of animals and knotty vegetables no one else would eat.

"I noticed something strange," Ellie said in a hushed tone to us, probably unnecessarily since we were at a table in the corner away from any break-taking employees. "There are exterior cameras all over this building. Every direction is covered. There are flood lights, too, next to each camera. Anything that happens outside the building, they must have on video, at least for the previous 24 hours."

"Flood lights only get about six to ten feet before the darkness swallows them up," Atari said. He was a big kid, as I have said, and he was really liking this "take what you want" open commissary. But he stopped shoveling as he thought, then said, "I wonder if you can see the tents from those cameras. That could be helpful."

"You guys sound like you're *actually* hunting cryptids," I said with a grin, one I wiped the hell off my face when I saw them each look at me with offended expressions.

"Uh, *yeah*," Ellie said, and I didn't like those gorgeous eyes looking at me like that, "that's what we *do*. What, do you think we just run around with our cameras and add breathless narration and then just edit together a bunch of nothing for the show?"

I blinked. That was exactly what I thought, of course.

Her voice was no longer hushed. "So because we've never caught an *Altamaha-ha* in focus on camera in broad daylight, that means it doesn't exist? Have you ever heard of the *okapi*, Mister Skeptic Asshole? Or the *komodo dragon*? These were both considered mythical creatures—*cryptids*, goddamnit—before they were finally documented and studied. Shit, the platypus was considered an *obvious hoax* when the explorers brought their carcasses back from Australia. An absence of evidence is *not* evidence of absence!"

There was nothing I could say, so I said nothing.

Gregory squinted at me and said, "Brother, if you don't support the mission, why are you even here? We could've hired a miner to hold the boom, paid him more than he would make in a year here."

"I *do* support the mission." I looked at each of them in turn—this was going to be a disaster if we weren't all on the same page—and tried to give them my most earnest look, the one I used to give my wife when she'd beg me to stop putting myself in danger. "I have gone after reported 'cryptids' all over the world, and all I've ever found are *rare* animals. *Endangered* animals that I help get relocated from this plague of humans eating up every inch of the wild. Yeah, I think your show is a lot of spectacle and not much substance. But that doesn't mean I'm not with you guys. We're going into the jungle tomorrow, in fact."

"Whoa!" Atari said, *just* as he was looking sympathetic to what I was saying. "Who put you in charge?"

"Sorry, sorry—*I'm* going into the jungle across the river tomorrow. During the day, even though it'll be dark as hell under the trees. You guys probably want to start by talking with the miners and getting their stories, right?"

Ellie had cooled down. "That's generally how we set the narrative, yes."

"So you guys go and do that and I'll do some recon in the jungle, see if I can find any sign of what we're actually dealing with here. Atari, maybe you can talk to Vermeulen's people tomorrow and determine what their security cameras can actually see. Then let's meet at five p.m. right here and compare notes."

Ellie nodded. Gregory nodded. But Atari just stared at me.

"What?"

"If you're a sound engineer, I'm the Queen of the Moon." He didn't crack a smile as he seemed to peer into me. I bet he was a damn fine cameraman with that kind of visual intensity. "So who are you, really? And what are you *using our show* for, man?"

I sighed. Of course I couldn't tell them who I worked for (or that I was working for anyone, in fact), but I could see my cover story was in tatters, so I decided not to exactly lie to them. I could give them *some* version of the truth. So I said, "That stuff I said about going all over the world, saving endangered animals?"

They all remained quiet.

"I'm independently wealthy, and I choose to spend my fortune—and my time—making the world a better place. I have people monitoring the Internet for chatter about bizarre or mythical animals—cryptids, as we call them, but to these people they are the *Chupacabra*, the Asian *Barmanou*, a *Black Shuck* or a *Megaconda*. To them, it really is an urban-legend goddamn *Man-Bear-Pig* that's eating their children and their pets or their milk-and-meat animals. Next thing you know, they're shooting or trapping and killing animals that are dangerous only because we took their territory. I save them. That's what I'm really doing here."

Atari whistled. "All right, man. That's noble. Thanks for the truth."

Ellie looked at me in a mischievous way, saying through her crooked smile, "I thought you had a little too much of the cock-of-the-walk about you for you just to be a sound man."

"Hey!" Gregory protested, mostly in jest.

"For him *just* to be a sound man. *Obviously* you have to be built to be holding that boom and carrying that equipment all the time. Your muscles are bigger than his, anyway."

I instinctively looked down at my arms. I had muscles, just not all show-off-y like his.

We finished our meal and tucked ourselves in inside the tent, the collegial feeling returned. Between killing three men right in front of them and then planning our day like the former commando I was, I had nobody to blame but myself for blowing my cover.

Since the last thing I saw before going to sleep for the night were Ellie's liquid green eyes fixed on me and her lips turned up in a sleepy smile, I wasn't too upset about the way things had worked out.

# CHAPTER 8

In the morning, we ate our high-calorie nutrition bars (Ellie cut hers in half, of course) drank a lot of water, and applied copious amounts of industrial bug spray over every exposed inch of skin. I strapped on my canteens; filled my rucksack with digital cameras, flashlights, rope, and a loaded tranquilizer gun; and pushed my two .45s into holsters that crisscrossed my chest like a *bandito*. I hate to kill animals, even non-endangered ones, even (believe it or not) humans, but if was going to be them or me, I would have to vote Team Brett.

Even though I wasn't going to play my part with the *Cryptids Alive!* scoobies, I was still glad they would be going about their plan for the show, interviewing everyone, getting lots of footage for the "B" roll, and generally acting like the TV production crew they were. This gave me the chance to see what the hell was going on, what kind of croc or team of predatory amphibious killers might be our miscreants.

I got permission from Vermeulen Mining to use one of their incredibly outdated flatboats to cross the slow current of the Kasai. The boat actually belonged to one of the longtime miners on the site, an impressive display of wealth among the barely-scraping-by tent city population, and he rented it to the company for a little extra cash every week. They rarely actually used it, but when you need to cross a river as big as this Congo tributary, you need to cross the river in a boat.

Or a floating whatever the hell this thing was. The friendly and wizened-looking miner—*gah, did this old man slip himself into those 50-foot-deep holes to dig for diamonds?*—told me in French, "Just push very hard with the oar and it will take you across. Use the oar if you need to not land downriver. Otherwise, just enjoy our Goddess River."

I gave him $4,500 in Congolese francs as thanks, and his nearly toothless mouth smiled widely at my generosity (in American dollars, it was about five bucks) and he wished me well on my journey across the water. He didn't ask why I wanted to go into the jungle—who knew why whites did anything, really? He probably assumed it was to find things to sell, since Americans cared only for what money could buy. The miners (and the rest of their ilk in Congo) liked money enough—eating and such being enjoyable—but, as a man in Ethiopia told me once, "Americans would seek money even if money could no longer buy anything." The super-rich one-percenters back in the States, sitting on their stacks of billions, made this poorest of poor men's statement stick with me.

In any case, five dollars later I was perched precariously in a boat that sat *in* the water, not just *on* it like a raft, keeping me on edge that the slightest sway would start it filling until it sank and I was in the middle of a river filled with lots of hungry things. A good shove with the oar, coupled by the old fellow getting his impressive muscle behind it, sent me halfway across the river before I needed to use the paddle of my oar to arrest getting caught up in the current and send more downriver than across it.

I needed to make just a few strokes, keeping my eyes peeled for crocodiles, hippopotami, and anything else that might feel my creeping boat was encroaching on their turf, and in just a few minutes I had made it to the far bank just a hundred yards or so from the smooth spot coming out of the jungle that was my main point of interest. I'd have to drag the boat upriver for the return journey, so hopefully I would end up landing at the right spot to return to the Vermeulen property.

This was really the first chance I'd had to be alone and take a good look at my surroundings—and any sign of where whatever creature we sought might have been making its home. The mud on this side was much more slippery and wet than I had expected from the mine side, but that was because I was forced to walk right at the waterline, the riot of vegetation threatening to push out over the river. However, after a couple of close calls that saw me very nearly lose my footing, I made it to what I was calling the "hole" in the jungle wall.

Holes like this, I knew, weren't created by one animal, even a large one, crossing to get into the river. No, this was either a frequently used path for river animals to come and go, or one hell of a big creature had blasted away the trees at this point as it rushed out of—or into—the dense jungle.

I peered around the corner of the hole, and as I had guessed, the brilliant sun ceased to provide much light past about ten feet in. I slowly eased myself around the foliage and into what I could now see was more of a tunnel than a hole.

If I had thought it was humid on the other side of river, far outside the dense jungle, then this was like being waterboarded. How could the air be so still and deathly stifling and yet so full of sound and movement. As soon as my eyes adjusted to the beams of sun filtered through the hundreds of feet of trees, vines, huge leaves, and everything else, I could see little animals—monkeys, rodents, massive insects both in the air and on the ground. The "ceiling" of this tunnel was at least ten feet high, plenty for me to walk upright, and it stretched further back than I could see in the gloom. I didn't touch a damned thing because I didn't want to pick up any kind of jungle rot or get bitten by something camouflaged on a tree trunk. Also, I didn't have to touch anything since this weird tunnel was so wide. There wasn't a human footprint or bootprint anywhere in the never-to-dry mud. Also, the edges of this "tunnel" were jagged, not what would have been the case if this had been manmade.

And despite the lack of any apparent human contribution to this cleared area, it *was* cleared. Which meant that something—or, more likely, some *things*—used this tunnel regularly, not giving the chaos of the jungle the opportunity to grow back and seal the gap, which would take no more than a month of neglect.

But *how* regularly? Were there human prints in the moist clay but which had been smeared out by the belly or feet or something huge? I crouched down to take a closer look at the mud I had been walking through. There were grooves in it, and the grooves were actually filled with water, telling me that whatever it was that made them came out of the river back into this jungle for some—

*HRRRRRRRGGGGGGGGGHHHHHHHH!*

I knew that sound, which was coming from about twenty feet behind me and froze me in place. It was the low, exhaling growl-roar of a very large crocodile. A few seconds later, it did it again, sounding wetter and angrier this time. I looked up and turned only my head as slowly as possible, and, sure as shit, there was a Nile crocodile staring at me. Staring at me and growling as it did first as a warning, then as an angry blast to petrify its prey, making it easier for the predator to chomp down and consume it.

I had some rope on me, and the tranq gun, and the two guns with bullets in it, but as the croc—an immense beast, this one bigger than the biggest saltwater man-eater I had even *heard* about—was facing me directly, shots to immobilize it or kill it would be impossible. Even the tranq gun couldn't pierce the tough skin on the croc's face. That part of the animal was protected to survive having another croc's jaws trying to crush it. If this one opened its mouth wide enough, I could shoot the tranq right into the softer tissue of its palate or tongue, but even then I would have to move enough to get that gun out of my bag that the croc would probably think I was about to flee, making him rush up and make me his screaming dinner.

I did turn my boots in the mud to bring my body around and better face the animal, on the off-off-chance that my staring it down would intimidate it and make it think twice about eating me. It let out another lion's growl and *hissed* as it opened its mouth at me, no doubt trying to gauge my reaction.

Wait, *hissed*? Crocodiles have a kind of hiss, I supposed, but it was more of a guttural exhalation than a snake's hiss. Yes, I thought, that sounded more like a snake's warning, not to mention that it came from behind me, not from the croc …

*Oh, bloody hell.* I turned my head again back to the direction I originally had it, looking into the jungle, not out at the river, which now seemed impossibly far away.

Staring at me from *this* side, about as far away as the croc was on the other, were the alien eyes of the largest snake I had ever seen. It didn't even look real, it was so huge. It was almost as tall as I was and seemed to stretch on forever. Was this the fabled cryptid *Megaconda*, essentially a monster-sized version of the already-monster-sized largest snake in the world?

It couldn't be. Anacondas, regular ones, didn't live in Africa, sticking with the smorgasbord available in South America's Amazon rainforest. No, this was Africa's version—the rock python. But it was impossible that a serpent of this size lived so close to humans. It would have been spotted! It would have been hunted and killed, definitely. Except the Vermeulen mine had set up shop right across the river no more than a year ago, moving from the previous site that it judged as holding no more diamonds.

I could have been the first person ever to see either of the creatures up close, never mind *both* of them. But that probably wasn't true, now that I thought about it while looking into the python's eyes, then looking behind me at the croc's, then back at the goddamned *basilisk* in front of me. Men may have seen these animals before, perhaps looking for food or wood in this part of the jungle, and were consumed immediately and entirely by one of these giant specimens. Hell, if a *regular*-sized Nile crocodile could corner you, he could swallow you in two bites. A normal rock python could coil around you so quickly your heart would be stopped before you even had a chance to cry for help. A normal rock python could also swallow a human whole.

And these were *not* normal-sized anythings. I couldn't call out for fear of prompting them to strike, and even if I did, no one would hear me through this dense jungle *and* across the river. And if even if *they* did, no one could come to my aid in time. So I didn't call out.

What I *did* do is stand very slowly, not only to try to look bigger but also to get some blood into my legs so I could be ready to make a theoretical run for it.

I couldn't outrun the crocodile on a wet, more-or-less smooth surface; and besides, that would be running right into the open maw of the Megapython. Similarly, there was no way in hell I could outrun even a regular python, let alone this beast; and again, that would put me right into the crocodile's waiting jaws.

*Rock, meet hard place.*

I sweated.

They licked their chops.

I was now officially out of time—the croc let out its angry roar now, the kind these animals always snarled right before they attacked, and I could see the gigantic python tensing to strike. I couldn't go forward, and I couldn't go back.

So I went sideways.

In two bounds, which each felt like they took half an hour, I leapt off the mud trail and into the trees and brush and God knows what on the right side of the muddy path. I couldn't run very far once I was in there because there were roots half my height blocking the way, but I had managed to barely slip between two trees right on the "tunnel," the largest gap I could have found in one hundred feet either way.

If I ever saw a church again, I would be stopping by to say thanks.

But it wasn't over. The crocodile, infuriated that this meal was trying to escape its deserving stomach, moved as fast as I had ever seen one go and swept right up the mud after me, slamming the very front of its snout between the two trees I had just squeezed through. It raged and roared and tired to push its way in, but it couldn't—and remember, these were a gap that just let a grown man with a rucksack on his back get through. The space was that large, and the steroid-rage giant crocodile could only get six inches of his snout through.

That is a goddamned giant-ass reptile.

But not as giant as the supersized rock python.

The snake's coiling to grab me, which I escaped by what I would estimate as exactly one second, wasn't intended to let it sweep to the side and gobble me as I tried to run away. If I had seen the gap and jumped even three seconds earlier, the python would have had time to haul me in or at least puncture me with a fang to hold me down while it squeezed me to death. And of course if I had jumped one second later, its spring would have forced me fatally down its throat before it even closed its mouth.

Like the Supercroc, the Megapython didn't quit either. It backed up its overshot and tensed in order to let it spring its massive bulk to the side this time, to where I had only just slipped between the trees and was a mere ten feet beyond the snout of the croc. It wasn't bluffing with that tensing, either, because it almost immediately swept to the side, slamming its huge scaly head against my two guardian trees so hard it made birds fly out a hundred feet above it.

It rammed its head against the trees and then quickly shut its jaw, driving its left fang right through the middle of the crocodile. The giant reptile shrieked and then released a roar that made me duck down even though I managed to crawl over one of the giant roots and get behind it. After that instinctive move, however, I brought my head back up over the root.

What I saw next I never would have believed if anyone claimed that *they'd* seen it. I completely forgot about the camera in my rucksack as I watched the python drag the croc away from the trees by that single enormous fang, then quickly (for a snake the length of two city buses, anyway) wrapped itself around the thrashing carnivore and *squeezed*. I could see the muscles tighten as it crushed the crocodile—itself almost as long as a single city bus—into stillness and, as its heart stopped, death.

Then the monster snake uncoiled itself from the mangled Nile crocodile and straightened out its long body. Then, not even needing to unhinge its massive jaw, it pushed forward and scooped the dead predator into its mouth and swallowed.

Its throat engorged, the Megapython coiled itself up again, getting into what I recognized as its resting position. It would take the snake maybe eight hours to fully swallow a meal of that size—I'm extrapolating from what happens when a regular-size Burmese python eats a regular-size alligator—so it would be staying exactly where it was for a while. I didn't dare come out from my safe spot, since for all I knew the Megapython would still have the energy, and the stomach capacity, to snag itself a second tasty morsel: *me*.

It was past three now. The sun was at an angle now where it made the jungle even darker. And this was the brightest it would be for the next 21 hours. The giant snake's eyes never closed, of course, and its gaze was fixed directly on me, where I believed it would remain until the crocodile was entirely digested. In a week or so.

I took my eyes off my jailer for the first extended time and looked all about me in the darkling jungle. The muddy path was the only reference I had to where I was in the jungle. I wanted to go further into the rainforest to get away from the Megapython, but I knew if I lost track of that opening onto the river, I would be as good as dead even without *literally* unbelievably enormous predators stalking me. There was one way out and one way in for all my intents and purposes: the hole in the jungle.

I would be sleeping against this massive tree tonight, it seemed. I would have to stay right where I was if I were going to live. My compass was small and I had no map or anything to make a map with. I could be within fifty feet of the muddy path and not see it. Unless I had a light on my compass and watched it every second— an impossibility when my eyes and attention were needed for navigating a ground seething with interwoven flora and fauna—I would quickly and inescapably veer off any straight path I was trying to forge and be lost. And that would be that.

I used my idle time to do something productive. I got the camera out of my rucksack and took picture after digital picture of the Megapython. I wished there were something in the frame for scale. I did what I could to establish the monster's size, taking parallax pictures that might give a sense of the thing in three dimensions. I did the same thing with the video setting, taking in the relative position of the snake against the backdrop of vines and trees and the foreground of the muddy path.

It was as good as pitch black a couple of hours after that, and, feeling enormous insects crawling near me and then on my body the entire time, hearing birds scream at one another along with the chittering of monkeys and the growls of God knew what, I slept as shallowly as I breathed, ready for any breath to be my last.

# CHAPTER 9

A susurration nearby made my eyes snap open. It was *dark* in the jungle, absolutely Stygian, but I had been in lightless forests and jungles many times. It was always uncomfortable, but I usually had lanterns and flashlights, not to mention companions who I could probably outrun if a bear came after us. Also, there usually wasn't a historically giant supersnake thirty or so feet away from me.

The rustling continued. Did I dare shine my flashlight? It could mean that whatever what was mucking about in the foliage—and, thank God, it sounded like it was on the other side of the mud path from me. I didn't know if the python was still there; it was so utterly dark that I literally could not see my hand in front of my face.

But now I actually could see a light behind and between the trees over there. Just the tiniest bit of light, and like looking at a dim star in the sky I could detect it only if I averted my gaze slightly and used only the rods in my peripheral vision. It flickered but stayed, and it was coming right from where the susurration had awakened me. I didn't know if hearing acuity improved when one couldn't see, but the light still seemed to be quite a distance away.

The birds had stopped chattering. I couldn't hear any monkeys jumping around the branches of the trees. Even the owls, thick in this part of Africa, weren't hooting. Usually these sounds were a constant background soundtrack, but now, for some reason, nothing moved, nothing peeped, nothing breathed.

I could look at the light directly now and see that it was the bobbling of a flashlight. I could hear the bearer—and obviously it was a human, maybe one looking for me—and maybe one companion making their rough way through the undergrowth. But soon the flashlight was pointing down at the wet clay and it became obvious they were treading a path familiar to them, which explained why they were able to move straight along, now obviously heading for the opening in the jungle that would take them to the lake. I hadn't heard them on their way in because they must have walked carefully and quietly when on the path.

They were about fifty feet away and I slowly stood up and grabbed my flashlight to signal them when an ear-splitting, tree-shaking, ground-rattling *ROAR* scared every bird and monkey and even insect into moving as fast as possible away from the sound.

It was like a lion's roar but at jet engine volume, with a spine-chilling *shriek* at the top of the register over the klaxon of the roar at the low end.

The two men—I assumed they were men from their whispered voices, giddy with fear—ran past with their flashlight. And I mean *ran*, even though I could see that the man not holding the flashlight was carrying something large and apparently quite heavy. From the bounce of the light's beam, I could see that the snake was still there but wasn't looking my way anymore, or even at the men as they raced by. No, even the Megapython, the biggest creature I or any other human had ever seen, looked toward the direction of the roar and coiled itself into a tight defense position, trying, it seemed, *to make itself look small.*

I was able to shake myself out of staring in that direction as well, turning to see the two men make it out of the foliage and almost immediately jump onto a waiting motorboat, which sped away out of my ken. It was again as dark as the abyss.

But there were sounds now, not only another titanic explosion of animal fury—amazingly, even louder and closer-feeling this time—but also thousands of every other kind of wildlife in that square mile of jungle screeching and running for its life.

Despite all of that noise, I could feel a rhythmic shaking of the ground even through my boots. Thoughts of *Jurassic Park* where the water in a cup in the tram car keeps rippling flashed through my head, but this shaking would have knocked that plastic cup right off the dashboard.

I didn't dare switch on my flashlight. All that would do—*ha! like with that girl in the movie!*—is attract not only the attention of whatever the hell was running at us, but also my old friend the Megapython. The snake, I knew, could see into the infrared, so it probably knew I was still there anyway, but in the one second that

I saw it in the men's flashlights I knew its attention had been diverted.

For that second, anyway. I was again completely blind in the utter dark and couldn't see what my hungry serpent was up to. I crouched down again behind my giant root where I had been sleeping, keeping just my eyes over the prominence in case anything suddenly became visible—

*HROAAAAAAAAAAAAAAAAAAAAAAAAAAAAAAAAAAAAAAAORR RRRR!*

I literally staggered back and fell on my ass. That came from almost right in front of—

*HISSSSSSSSSSSSSSSSSSSSSSSSSSSSSSSSSSSSSSSSSSSSSSSSSSSSS SSSSSSSSSSSSSSSS!*

"*Jesus!*" I barked out loud, then clamped both hands over my mouth like in a pantomime show. That *hiss* was the Megapython, it had to be. It was as loud as a locomotive's whistle—but still didn't even approach the other thing's raging roar.

I regained my footing and looked out at the unilluminated scene which sounded like it was taking place before me. It was pitch black still, and even the screams of the snake and the crocodile-like snarls (times a thousand decibels) of the other didn't make them any more visible.

*BOOM!* The ground shook so hard a tree fell a few meters behind me.

Then there was a wet *crunch* and the sound of *tons* of meat being chewed and swallowed. Finally that stopped and after hearing a massive *squelching* noise, I jumped back as something that felt like the size of a boulder slammed into those two trees that had just barely allowed me entrance into my hollow. Branches and monkeys rained down all around of me, judging by the sound.

But it was not over. This creature, whatever it was, let out another air-rending roar of fury and ran off down the path, sliding right into the Kasai and vanishing.

A few minutes later, maybe less, I could hear human screams from across the river as well as the unholy sound of whatever had gone into the river and come out on the other side, on the mine's side.

To this day, I don't believe that I passed out. I think my body and my mind just quit. They could take no more of the impossible and simply shut down, leaving me to fall into a deep slumber against the giant root.

# CHAPTER 10

I awoke in layers of sensation. First was a symphony of animal sounds, a nice and normal jungle cacophony. Then a million spots of light sparkled against my eyelids as the daylight streamed through the treetops. I could next feel my sweaty and completely filthy and bug-bitten body itching like hell and taste jungle rot in my mouth.

But the smell—the *stench*—was what finally aroused me to consciousness. I opened my eyes and coughed at the foulness. I waved a cloud of gnats away from my face and stood to see what was on the other side of—

"*HOLY SHIT!*" I yelped, and if my heart had simply exploded at that moment, it wouldn't have been at all surprising. I caught my breath as I looked into the 15-foot-wide mouth of the Megapython, its dead forked tongue hanging out the side because the snake's head was at about a 45-degree angle to the ground. Its eyes were flat instead of bulbous. Which is what happens when blood ceases to exert pressure in an animal's body.

Still recovering my senses after shrieking like a very foul-mouthed little girl, I saw the reason for the python's lack of blood pressure: it was only the monster's head that had been hurled at trees, probably when whatever ate everything between that head and the length of tail in the bushes on the other side was shaking it violently in its unimaginably massive jaws. (As in I could not even imagine how massive those jaws would have had to be in order to bite right through a 15-foot-in-diameter serpent *that had just eaten the largest crocodile ever seen.*)

The monster, which was bigger than this monster, which was in turn bigger than the monster *it* had eaten, hadn't gobbled the serpent whole or slurped it down like a noodle, but that was probably because the snake presented its flank sometime during their earthshaking battle royale.

Making 360-degree sweeps of my immediate environment by turning every step or two, I was able to get right next to the overwhelming decay smell of the Megapython, already full of every kind of carrion insect in the jungle and stinking like the devil's asshole even though it had been dead ten hours at the very most. I was dazed as hell from sleeping—hell, passed out—in the jungle, but I had to see the enormous snake head close up to check that my sanity hadn't been lost through an exotic insect's venom. Then, walking *very* carefully and still making those full circles to spot any supra-apes bigger than King Kong or colossal wasps the size of a WWII bomber, I examined what remained of the python's tail. Then I looked around again. I could see the opening out onto the Kasai River, so close and yet so very far away. I waited at that spot near the snake's tail, waited and listened and watched for anything that might come to pop me in its mouth like I was a Tic-Tac.

After a few minutes, I felt reasonably confident that there was now just the normal African rainforest jungle of incredible, but *normal*, danger. If I weren't smelling the remains of my Megapython, I could almost have believed it was a dream I had after collapsing from the heat and humidity. But it wasn't. And now it was time to walk out the way I had walked in and see what thoroughly unbelievable horror had occurred in the tent city the night before.

***

"My God," I murmured under my breath as I reached the edge of the jungle, where I could see flattened tents, mangled bodies, and lots of smoke. It was a little after 8:00 in the morning. As I paddled across the river, I couldn't see a single person moving in the entire mining site. I saw the *Cryptids Alive!* tent on its rise. It seemed undamaged, but I didn't see any of the crew moving around inside or out. I landed the flatboat more or less where I had intended and tied it off.

As I walked up the bank, I wondered: had the mud been smoothed on this side of the river yesterday? Or was it caused by some gigantic creature slithering out of the green river? I wished I had bothered to take notice of this yesterday, but I had honestly thought I was going to check out where a croc had laid its eggs near the opposite waterline or the like. Not that was about to step onto the set of *Land of the Lost*.

There were, as reported in the dossier given to me by my Boss, pieces of bodies here and there, an arm, a head, a torso without any extremities at all. Tents mashed onto fires were what was burning and throwing the smoke into the air. But only a dozen or so tents looked like they had been stepped on and there were "only" ten or twenty people killed as represented by the body parts strewn around. Where was everybody else?

I looked up and almost literally slapped my hand to my forehead: *the bunker*. Vermeulen Mining had that huge area, more than half of its concrete building, in which to hide its workers during an attack. It seemed that those who could make it to the building by the time the *thing* pounded on the door and were saved. The ones closest to the mine and the river couldn't get away in time.

Was that what the two men I saw by the light of their own flashlights doing there last night, running to warn the miners that *something* was coming? Even with a motorboat, they would have had a hard time beating the swimming beast across the river. There was no sign of a motorboat this morning. Had they not made it, or had they made it in time to wake almost everyone and herd them into the bunker? Had the creature destroyed their boat as it climbed out of the river, or did they survive to drive it away?

And if they did drive away ... *why*? Maybe they did it so they could send up flares or something to awaken the miners so didn't even land the boat on that shore? And if that was what happened, where the hell did they *go*?

Filthy, with bugs in my hair, sweating on top of the sour sweat already seeped deep into my clothes, I made it to the front door of the Vermeulen Mining building and banged on it as hard as I could in my confused, fried condition.

After a minute or so, a buzzer sounded and the door opened. Ellie White's face popped out and she yanked me in by my sleeve as the door closed, right into an embrace so tight I couldn't help but think of the Megapython. "You're alive!" she shouted with amazement in her voice. "You went into the jungle and never came out—we thought you were dead, especially after—"

She took in a huge gasp and held me at arm's length, taking me in with wild eyes.

"—the *Kasai Rex!* It attacked last night! They were able to get almost all of the miners inside in time, but holy crap, Brett! It *does* exist!"

Atari and Gregory had come over now to join her and slap me on the back like I had just become a father. My eyes were adjusting to the lower light level inside the compound now, and I saw many black faces poking out of sleeping bags with "Property of Vermeulen" printed on the side. I looked back at her and the rest of the crew and stammered, "D-Did you get any footage? What did it look like? *What the hell was it?*"

Ellie let loose her grasp on my arms and all three of them looked sheepishly at the floor as Atari said, "We didn't exactly get any video."

"Or audio," Gregory muttered.

"I was uploading the B-roll and interviews to the sat-link. We didn't have the cameras out of the cases. We didn't think something would happen so *soon*," Atari added. "And it was really dark."

"The only lights were those pathetic floodlights on this building. You couldn't see a damned thing farther than five feet from the building," Gregory said.

"It was really, really dark." Atari looked at me and shrugged. "You bet your butt I'll have the infrared set up as soon as the sun even thinks about going down from now on."

"We didn't *see* anything, Brett," Ellie said quietly, "but we *heard* everything. It was terrible."

"Mister Russell," a Dutch accent resounded, and Daan Vermeulen, already in a different sharp gray suit, joined our group and shook my hand. "You look like you had a rough night out there. I'm glad you're all right, to say the least. I trust you found something out there that might be able to help us with our problem?"

"I don't know exactly what I found out there," I said. "But I need a shower and some breakfast before I tell you all what happened. You're not going to believe it."

***

Almost an hour later, as I wiped up yolk remains with a piece of wheat toast and watched as the last of the miners emptied out of the building and back to work—including discarding their fellows' body parts into the Kasai, I had to assume—Daan Vermeulen sat back and said, "You are right, Mister Russell. I *don't* believe it."

"I had video and some parallax photos."

"But you forgot your backpack in the jungle."

"By the time I realized it, I was halfway across the river coming back."

"So you could go and retrieve it."

There was no amount of money or glory that would have compelled me to go back into that mutant-giant hole of horrors. "No, the monkeys have probably already run off with it and dumped everything along the way," I said after a moment, knowing it sounded lame but also knowing that it was the truth.

"I see." Vermeulen smoothed his already-smooth tie and turned to Ellie. "And you and the rest of your crew didn't have your equipment ready to capture this beast on video." It wasn't a question. More of a pouring-salt-on-an-open-wound kind of sentence.

"We had an opportunity last night that may not come again, Mister Vermeulen, we understand that," she said. "But all we can do now is set up our night-vision equipment and hope it happens again. Um, I mean, of course I don't hope for anyone else to die or—"

Vermeulen laughed the single least amused-sounding laugh I had heard since my own at the funeral for my wife and boy, when some third-cousin or somebody said, "At least they're in Heaven now."

*Heh.* Good one.

After Vermeulen's chuckle, he stood and said, "I believe you will find out what's killing our people, Miss White. I have to. None of my employees or miners will go to explore that black hole Mister Russell went into yesterday, not for any amount of money I offered them. 'Money is hard to spend when you're dead,' the miners say, and my office workers here are comfortable in their hidey holes. Good day to you all. I must tally up last night's losses."

Ellie nodded at him and then, seeing the janitorial crew rolling up the sleeping bags for laundering or storage, called to his retreating figure, "The monster attacks only at night, isn't that what you said?"

Vermeulen turned with a perturbed look on his face and came back to our table to say in a low growl, "I'll thank you not to call it a *monster*, Miss White. And yes, whatever it is, it has come at night, only at night."

"Then … why don't you just let your miners sleep inside here in the sleeping bags every night? No one mines during the night, right? It's hard enough when there's light."

Vermeulen stiffened and I knew something completely awful was about to come out of his mouth, something the *Cryptids Alive!* crew and I would laugh and shake our heads about back in our big tent but ultimately wish we had never heard. That sounds ridiculously specific, but you didn't see the look on his face, like his foie gras had been replaced with goose shit.

He said, "My employees have quarters in this building, you must realize. They eat here, work here, sleep here, enjoy whatever amusements keep them sane until their 'tour of duty' is over. They—especially the women who make up the bulk of my office workforce—wouldn't feel comfortable with that many, em …"

"Negroes?" Atari offered with a straight face it must have been hard to maintain.

"… with that many *indigenous people* having access to the building all night. It's a matter of safety, you see."

"Oh, we see," Gregory said. "I'm surprised you let our cameraman eat in the commissary here."

"Don't be absurd," Vermeulen said, and set off to leave again. But before he literally turned on his heel and fled our piercing stares, he added, "This isn't about *race*. It's about *safety* for everyone. We let them in if there's a crisis. That is quite enough."

And he was gone.

"Whew, for a second there I thought racism might have been about *race*," Atari said, and we all enjoyed a bitter laugh. Then he leaned toward me and said, "*Is* it true, what you said? About the giant crocodile, the gianter python, and the even-gianter super-monster?"

"It's all true, I swear. There's no reason for me to lie about this, to you or to anyone else."

"That means you've seen with your own eyes *three* cryptids, while we have never gotten a good look at even *one* during our show's entire run?" Ellie said, defying me to stick to my story.

"I only *saw* two of them. The last one, the leviathan, it was too dark, but I could hear it eating the Megapython. And I could see the two men running out of there because of their flashlights."

Ellie sat up straighter. "You didn't say anything about any other people in there. You told him and us this entire freaking story without *once* mentioning anyone else. What were they doing, these men who have suddenly appeared in your little narrative?"

"Just running. They looked like they knew exactly where they were going, too, so they must have been through that area many times to navigate it while running, even with a flashlight." I thought for a moment, then added, "They took off in a motorboat before the giant whatever-it-was came through. It might have caught them if it hadn't stopped to eat the snake, especially since one of the men was slowing them down. He was carrying something heavy, I could tell from his gait as his flashlight swung back and forth."

"Impressive detail," Ellie said. "What an imagination on our poacher hunter."

"If this is all fantasy and lies on my part, then what attacked the miners last night? Or do you think that's all 'suddenly appeared' in my narrative as well."

Ellie sucked in one of her red lips and looked at Atari and Gregory, then returned to look at me. "All right," she said, "now we've got us a mystery to go with our monster. While the sun's still up, I'm going into that hole across the river—and *I'm* not going to forget the camera."

"I knew she was gonna say that," Atari said with a sardonic smile.

"As did I," said Gregory.

"You guys do whatever you want. But before I go anywhere near that hole again, I'm getting back to that Jeep that Bonte blew up. We're going to need that thing they had mounted on the windshield."

"What, the machine gun?" Atari asked as I stood.

"That's a 105mm M40 recoilless rifle, kids." They all looked at me, perplexed. So I added, "It kills *tanks*."

# CHAPTER 11

The mines were the midst of the Congolese rainforest, a riot of living, crawling, growing *life*. Not only was it supplied with water from its deep—itself filled with plants and animals not yet named by scientists—but it also blossomed thunderstorms almost 230 days per year. And a Congo thunderstorm isn't like a New England gully washer. No, it's a nearly solid thing, the rain not in sheets but as a brick wall descending on you, full of close-striking lightning and with thunder that shears the air.

Ellie, Atari, Gregory, and I had made it halfway to our tent when the sky opened up like it has been slashed with a razor. "Join hands!" I shouted just before the world went gray with rain so thick and loud none of us could have found the others if they weren't connected to them. Lightning made us crouch low in what was probably a vain attempt to not become human lightning rods and kept going in the direction we had started in, toward the tent.

The rain wasn't just heavy as a downpour—it was *heavy*, a billion huge and warm drops making an actual weight upon our shoulders and heads. I was exhausted from the night before, but the shower and food had perked me up. Maneuvering through this rain and explosive lightning and thunder was enervating me once again, and I needed every bit of strength and clear thinking I could muster. By the time our tent appeared out of the rain—Ellie led the way and hit the bullseye, and we all piled in gratefully.

"You're good at this," I managed to wheeze inside the tent. That was something I had forgotten about rainforest storms: there was no *air*. It was like being submerged—you had to hold your breath if you didn't want lungs full of water. So we all sucked in as much oxygen as we could inside the fancy-ass tent, hyperventilating before we could slow ourselves down and breathe more or less normally.

As if there hadn't been almost a full minute since I used the last of my breath to compliment here, Ellie whipped her wet hair back and out of her face. "I know you think *Cryptids Alive!* is bullshit—lots of people do, including some of our biggest fans—but if we weren't really trying to see what's out there, we could do the show in front of a green screen and in the woods right next to our studio parking lot."

"I get you, okay?"

"What I'm saying is that I learned some things out there looking for amazing animals."

I nodded and continued breathing rhythmically, trying to get the last of the black spots out of my field of vision, then said, "After last night, I am officially no longer a skeptic."

The trio laughed, but it was true—unless I had gone insane and hallucinated from rubbing against the wrong plant while in that tiny edge of the Congo jungle, I saw things the night before that would forever change me. Did these "cryptids"— I use the quotes because once an unusual animal is discovered and verified, it ceases to be labeled as cryptic—count as endangered or rare species for the purposes of my job here?

It was time to contact The Organization. I looked at my (thankfully totally waterproof) watch and figured it was the middle of the day back in Denver. It wouldn't have mattered—they picked up the phone day or night, and nothing is entrusted to an answering service. I borrowed the sat-phone and moved to a corner of one of the big tent's "rooms," which wouldn't provide much in the way of privacy but could at least allow my end of the conversation to be drowned out a little by the storm. I chucked off my soaked shirt and pants and sat.

The phone connected, but its signal was too garbled by the rain and lightning to convey voices. I switched it over to text, which would read out on the sat-phone's small screen. It wasn't ideal— the Boss didn't care for a paper trail, even one as temporary and unarchiveable as the phosphorous letters on a 5-inch screen in Africa. I'm just gonna tell relate our text conversation like a regular conversation to help protect the sanity of whomever might read this. Nobody "said" anything out loud, but boy, were some things said over the satellite phone's text connection.

"Hello, H———," the Boss said as the secure connection was made. "I imagine this is something important?"

"Of course, sir … unless you just want to chat."

"Funny. What's your report? Did you find a saltwater croc? Before you answer, let me remind you that The Organization is not relocating an animal of 'least concern.'"

"I found a croc, of sorts. It had all the features of a Nile crocodile but was *much* bigger than anything ever reported."

"I see." And I knew what he was "seeing." It was a very large crocodile, maybe of unprecedented size—he knew what Congo was like and that it could easily hold such a reptile. "You aren't contacting me over a sizeable, and non-endangered, animal of unusual size, are you? If the answer is that you *are*, you should immediately pretend that the satellite lost your signal."

"I'm not. And it hasn't."

"What, then?"

I paused. "In the jungle, I came across a python. A *huge* rock python that, um ... well, it swallowed the giant croc in two gulps."

Silence on the Boss's end.

"It was 15 feet across if it was an inch," I said. "It was bigger than the Megaconda is supposed to be, sir."

"The Megaconda is a cryptid, H. As in, nobody's ever really seen one. Are you telling me that you actually saw and photographed a Megapython?"

*Shit.* "I did, but my camera was lost in my scramble to get away."

"I see," he said again. And I knew again what he was "seeing."

"I could return to that part of the jungle and try to find the camera, but I'm sure that monkeys and other scavengers have run off with it by now."

"Convenient."

I did an actual double-take at the screen I was reading from. Was that *sarcasm*? In my twelve years in The Organization, the Boss had never spoken to me like that. However, it was difficult to get tone from just typed words, and of course, I had never said I actually *saw* a cryptid creature that natives reported stole their valuable animals and less financially valuable but probably still beloved children. I tried to shake the Boss's apparent tone out of my head, then said, "Also, sir, the giant snake was also attacked and almost entirely eaten by another predator."

"*Another predator*, you say. As in 'something large enough to eat a 15-foot-wide Megapython that had just eaten the world's largest crocodile.'"

"I know it sounds absurd, but—"

"You're goddamn right it sounds absurd, because it *is* absurd. Have you been out in the field so long you've forgotten our mission? It isn't to find amusing variations of animals to report to the Royal Academy of Science. You're not Richard Francis Burton, H————; you're not seeking the source of the Kasai. The Organization needs you to *focus* like you have always done. Find the endangered animal terrorizing the poor bastards in the village and get it relocated."

"I understand our mission, sir—"

"I don't think you do. I think you *have* forgotten our mission." He paused for any response from me—which was not forthcoming, as I had no idea what to say to his accusation—then continued, "In fact, tell me our mission. Tell me what you think it is. Forget about what's on the front of our portfolios—tell me what our mission *really* is."

This conversation was going from bad to worse, and it wasn't done. I took a moment, possibly infuriating the boss with my lassitude regarding his question, but I needed a smoke, the *Cryptids Alive!* crew with their sensitive lungs be damned. I slipped a cheroot out of its (thankfully) waterproof liner from my front pocket and struck a match from another liner in my back pocket, lighting my little stick of happiness before shaking the match out and putting it in the tin cup which was now promoted to ashtray status.

"That wasn't a request, H."

"If I'm not mistaken, sir, and everything is upside-down right now, it is 'to protect endangered wildlife by removing—'"

"I said the *real* one, you asshole. Are you trying to test my patience? Because you're doing an excellent job ... at *that*, at least. Now what is our goddamned mission? Show me you know it before I cut off your funds and you and your TV pals have to walk back to the U.S."

I had never heard him like this. I took a shaky draw on the cheroot and exhaled as I said, "We protect indigenous populations encroaching on virgin territory by removing—"

"*Forget about the goddamned animals!* Do you not even *know* our mission? All these years and it's never occurred to you?"

"Sir, I'm sorry. I don't have even the slightest idea what you're talking about." I gulped and realized how dry my throat was, ironic since I was still soaked from the run to the tent. "No one's ever told me I was doing anything wrong. I mean, you're the only other member I even know. If you didn't tell me, then I don't know."

A big sigh came from his end of the sat-phone. "This adventure of yours is so goddamn sideways at this point, it won't hurt to tell you explicitly what you've done all these years."

My heart was already pounding in my chest, and it didn't slow down at the Boss's latest words. I had dedicated my *life* to The Organization after my wife and boy died in the firebombing. Twenty-four hours a day, seven days a week, as many hours in a day as I could stay awake. It had been *four years*, and two years before my family was killed. No, I wasn't available at the drop of a hat when they had been alive, but I served The Organization well and they compensated me just as well. Was the Boss saying I had no idea what I was doing all these years? Was I *not* saving endangered species, *not* protecting indigenous people who reported cryptid predators? I choked out, "Then tell me."

You know how you can hear someone smile as they're talking sometimes? Yeah, this was that: "H————, saving children and goats and what-have-you is noble, as is risking your life to catch poachers and save endangered predators."

*Predators?* Yes, I supposed it almost always was a predator of the "most concern" variety, but that was what got in the news, people telling stories about legendary creatures eating things and doing things that scare the piss out of people living hand-to-mouth, whether it was next to a river or in the middle of a desert. So predators. "Yes, I always thought it was a noble way to make a buck," I said. "I've never lost any sleep at night. Except last night."

"Excellent. Now, in any of those dozens, maybe over a hundred adventures out in the wilds, whether with recruited poachers, or being sent in undercover like this time, or doing it by yourself with just a guide, have you *ever* reported a real cryptid of any kind? I'm not talking about a new species of hedgehog or some ridiculous orchid. I'm talking about the predators, the *big* game."

"You know I haven't."

"Exactly, exactly." He continued like a math professor explaining how functions worked to a class full of football players. "And out of those, let's say, one hundred adventures, how many successfully relocated an endangered predator, one near the top of the near-extinction list?"

"I keep track, sir. It's been 93 animals, so 93 percent if there were one hundred adventures. A pretty good record, I think."

"Indeed, as I've told you many times, you're our best operative. Or were. You're reporting cryptids now, giant crocodiles and even more giant snakes. And please tell me, was it an actual *Kasai Rex* who ate the snake?"

"And killed several miners," I added. "But I don't know what attacked—it was too dark."

"I see. No pun intended."

"Very droll, sir. Listen, sir, I called you because there is some unprecedented wildlife lurking in this area. The biggest of the specimens, I believe, has been attacking the miners, killing many of them and forcing the rest into the company building for safety, even if that's only temporarily and if they can make it in time."

A harsher tone entered the Boss's voice: "What? Who is letting them into that building?"

I stammered for a second, not expecting him to say anything like *that*. "I—uh—I guess some of the Vermeulen employees who live in the building?"

"That soft piece of shit," he said, almost making my head spin. Was I going insane, as I thought last night, from some bug bite or poisonous mushroom spore? Or was *he* losing his mind? The things he was saying … my little room in the tent seemed claustrophobic now. The rain continued to beat down, as it would for another hour at least. "That son of a bitch!"

"Wow, sir, I don't know what to—"

"This isn't the Special Forces anymore, boy. You don't just get objectives handed to you. You need to know our *mission*. And, since you seem not to have any goddamned idea, let me share it with you: *We provide what our customers pay for.* And what do they pay for, you're about to ask. They pay for absolute security, complete immunity from prosecution, and total freedom to do whatever the hell they want."

Nothing. I had nothing.

"What do they pay? Two to five million dollars per hunt. *Million*, H————. Our clients, our customers, are the richest men and women in the world. Our fee is practically a rounding error to them. Our *mission*, you dolt, is to give them their *substantial* money's worth."

"Per *hunt*?" I had to be in a nightmare and shook my head to try to wake myself up, but in the nightmare I remained. "I think I might have misheard you, s—"

"You did not. The endangered creatures we relocate go to an undisclosed location that varies depending on what kind of environment the animals need. Then our clients go in and kill those animals for trophies. Every amenity is seen to, every legal technicality exploited. Our mission is to keep them supplied with game, with animals no one else may ever hunt again. Imagine possessing the last dodo ever shot, or the last Tasmanian tiger? They pay to make history. In secret, of course, but history nonetheless."

"I feel sick."

"Anyone would feel sick in your shoes," the Boss said, not unkindly, but then added, *extremely* unkindly: "You're a moron not to have seen what you allowed The Organization to do, Mister Special Forces, but you're a damned good soldier. You have been our number one since you started. Even more valuable since your misfortune. One day you'll catch the poachers who did that to your family, right? Isn't that what you've always believed?"

"What in the *hell* are you talking about?"

"*We're* the poachers! You and I and the entire Organization are the poachers. And when you couldn't do as much poaching as we needed you to do ... well, we poached your family, didn't we?"

I tried to speak but no sound was possible.

"That really upped your productivity, I must say. I bet you wonder why I'm telling you all of this now."

"You could say that," I rasped, my eyes seeing nothing but red.

"Because you're fired, son. You've seen real cryptids now, haven't you?"

"Yes."

"You believe in them now."

"Yes."

"We don't need any true believers on our team, H————. We need the best poachers in the world, the ones who can take out other poachers so we can serve our high-living clientele, not the ones who know about the secret creatures of our planet. Those can't be killed by our customers—too big, their behaviors too unknown. It makes me sad. You were the very best, and I'm sorry to see you go. But you did your family proud—"

"*Don't you talk about my family, you bastard—*"

"Yes, yes, let it out. A large severance check will be headed to a post office box in Denver where you can pick it up."

"I'll rip it up."

"I doubt you will. Destroy a clue as you try to hunt me down? Refuse the money that would aid you in your futile search? I don't see that happening."

"I *will* find you and I *will* kill you."

"Maybe so! You are the most prolific poacher in the world, after all. Until then, have fun in Congo. Your plane tickets back home, dated for tomorrow evening; your apartment lease; your driver's license; all will be under 'Brett Russell' *very* shortly and delivered to Daan Vermeulen tomorrow morning—and at great expense, I might add. But it's worth it: lots of angry, heavily armed, recently released former poachers would love to find 'Brett Russell,' so do watch your step."

"*I will kill you.*"

"All right, you're repeating yourself now, *Brett*. Have fun with your Kasai Rex or whatever else you think you saw in the jungle." The connection ended, a single appearing almost to float in white against the black background: ——-CONNECTION TERMINATED——-.

I shut down the phone, and a minute later Ellie scratched on the synthetic fabric of the wall, the only way to "knock" inside our tent. She almost recoiled when she saw my pallor and teary eyes, not to mention me sitting there in my boxers by the sat-phone. "Oh my God, are you okay?"

"You can see damn well I'm not, but I appreciate you asking."

She knelt down beside me sitting on the floor and put an arm around me. The rain sounded peaceful now, even though it was pounding the tent as hard as ever. "Tell me, Brett. Tell me whatever you want. You don't have to carry this alone … whatever it is." She kissed me gently on each eye, and then sweetly on my lips.

Maybe just everything felt more peaceful when Ellie had her arm around me, kissing me and inviting me to cry on her shoulder. Damn it all to hell, I told her everything. *Everything*. The Organization had thrown me away like paper wiped on its ass. I didn't have to keep their secrets anymore, or mine.

When I was finished talking and weeping and clenching my fists against her back in anger and despair, she used my soaked shirt collar to wipe my face, she kissed me. Then she said, "Tell me something about your wife."

"What?"

"Share a memory of your wife. Keep her alive, if only between us."

I was as surprised as hell at Ellie's gentleness, her *femininity*, since I had seen her scream like a banshee in the face of danger and lash out to hurt one would hurt her as suddenly and as naturally as a cat. The feeling of surprise was a happy one, so I thought for a moment and answered her request: "Jenny wrinkled her nose when she laughed. Whenever we'd hear that Sinatra song, the super-romantic one, we'd laugh when he'd sing"—and I sang it:

♪ *And that laugh that wrinkles your nose …* ♪

"… we'd crack up, and her laugh would wrinkle her nose all over again! She turned *so* red."

We laughed together, still touching, never louder than the rain, as if it were just us in that tent and nothing else anywhere that could ever hurt us. But I knew what was next.

"And your son?"

It took me a second to make sure I could say his name out loud. "Harry."

"Harry Potter fans, huh?"

I shook my head and said, "It was Harry Junior. That's my name." I thought to the terrible text call with the Boss. "It *was*. It isn't anymore. Now I'm Brett."

"Tell me something about Harry Junior."

"He loved dinosaurs, like most boys his age, I guess. But he would spend hours reading the books about them and watching documentaries—heh, on the History Channel, come to think of it. He would color them in coloring books with their names at the bottom. Of course the *T. Rex*, but also the stegosaurus, the mosasaur, the spinosaurus—which fought the tyrannosaurus for food, and most always won. At least, that's what my little expert told me." I wiped away a tear before it reached the smile my memory had created. "God, he used to spiel fact after fact about every dinosaur—how it hunted, where it lived, what kind of 'family' structure the species had. And he was *eight!* He was only eight ..." I didn't wipe away the fresh tears.

"That's *yours* now. Nobody can take that from you. And you can be the hero I bet your son thought you were. You can still do so much good here. You can save the miners."

I initiated our kiss this time. Her lips were as tender as her heart. "Maybe," I said, letting out a breath that could have been a laugh or could have been a sigh of resignation, or both. But Ellie turned my face toward hers, not to kiss me again, but to fix me with a smile and then a stern look.

"But first, we need that gun."

# CHAPTER 12

Ellie and I got up and walked into the "living room" of the tent, where Gregory were fiddling with equipment that did look loosely grouped by "video" and "audio." I brought the sat-phone back in with me and set it down between them, let the techies work it out.

Atari came out of one of the other "bedrooms" of the tent and sniffed the air. "Something burning?"

"Sorry," I said. "Had a cigar in there. I was having ... some stress."

"I hear ya," he said. "I hate when we go international. I can't exactly bring my 'stress reducing' smoke on the plane, if you get me."

"We get you, pothead," Gregory said, and they laughed. "Where'd you go off to, anyway?"

Atari said with a show of injured pride, "I was meditating."

Eyebrows went up all around the room.

"What, a brother can't meditate? Enlightenment is reserved for the Chinese and white people?" he said with a serious face that turned into a new smile.

I said, "I got to ask you guys a question. It sounds weird, but ... did the History Channel supply you with round-trip tickets?" I gave them each a look that showed as weird as the question may have been, I was asking it in earnest.

"Yeah, they always do," Atari said. "I mean, we have to have flexible dates for the return—we never know what we're gonna run into—but they take care of all that stuff."

"I know there has to be a good reason you're asking us," Ellie said, and she was right.

"My ticket was just changed by my now-*former* boss. I have to fly out tomorrow afternoon or I'm not getting home. All my financial information is being switched to an identity I don't have yet. I won't be able to access a dime until I can go to my bank and broker in person back in the States."

Their jaws couldn't have dropped and farther. "They *fired* you?" Atari said, distress in his voice. "What the hell *for*?"

"It doesn't matter," I said. "What matters is that there's a giant *something* out there, and it's going to keep attacking these poor bastards unless we stop it. Are your cameras and such waterproof?"

"Yes, we film around rivers and lakes—it's all baffled and protected," Gregory said, showing me his microphone setup. I don't know how we picked up any sound with it like that, but apparently he could.

"Great. Because tonight might be our one chance to stop this … cryptid."

Ellie protested, "That's not enough time—we've got to wait for the rain to stop to get the machine gun off the Jeep, *if* it's even still there. And get back, *and* set up the cameras and mics—"

"We don't have to wait until the rain stops," Atari said with a smile.

"Yes, we do!" Ellie snapped. "This frickin' *deluge* hasn't let up. You can barely see two feet in front of you! How are we supposed to find that Jeep?"

"Infrared, boss lady. It can see right through the rain. I mean, not all the way to that Jeep, but enough that we can navigate by closer landmarks one by one until we get there."

"We have to do this tonight?" Ellie asked me.

"We really *should* do it under the cover of the rain," Atari said, and ducked back into his room for a moment, coming back out with a very-well-protected–looking piece of camera equipment. "If it's anything to do with tech, I got it down."

"I leave tomorrow unless I want to become a Congolese miner myself. They're probably spending $2,000 to get my ticket here in time to force me to leave tomorrow afternoon."

"Why don't they just do it electronically?"

"My former employer is no fool. He's sending the new ticket—the old one being removed from any airline system, I'm sure—under my new name, the one you guys know me as: Brett Russell. He's also included all the ID I need to get on a plane with a ticket for a 'Brett Russell.'"

"What an asshole," Gregory said.

"So yeah, we have to do this tonight if I'm to help *Cryptids Alive!* get its scoop."

We all smiled at that, and Atari, already in his rain poncho, held up the infrared camera and cheered, "Let's do th—"

He was cut off by the tent "door" unzipping and our old friend Bonte sticking his head in, beads of rain all over his slight afro. We all greeted him pretty happily, but he looked like someone who had just lost his best friend. "Misters and Miss, the big boss wants to see you. Mister Vermeulen. He says *now*."

We all looked at one another, nobody saying anything.

"*Now*, he says," Bonte repeated, and pulled his head back out. Rain whipped in where he left the door unzipped.

"*Now, he says*," Atari said in Bonte's accent, then Ellie repeated it, the Gregory, then me. It was a bit of gallows humor as we put dry gear on and went back out into the maelstrom and our uncertain fate.

***

Daan Vermeulen, who was not wet, stood waiting for us in the middle of the large empty part of the mining company's bunker. We bedraggled travelers, soaked with rain and mud, walked over to where he was, dripping and splashing all the way. Obviously he didn't want his precious office carpet messed up, not if his white employees would be expected to walk on it.

He didn't say hello and so neither did we. He did say, "I would like to invite your team to sleep inside this building tonight. We have a couple of spare rooms, two beds each. You won't have to stay on the concrete floor out here in a sleeping bag."

"Thank you," Ellie said, although I could feel her wanting to say something about how the concrete was good enough for the miners. But she kept her cool.

"My pleasure, Miss White," he said, then added, "I should tell you to bring everything you might need overnight into the building with you, and of course your expensive equipment shouldn't be left even in a tent. The miners might be too tempted."

"Nice," Atari said.

"Shut your mouth, boy. For all I care, you can sleep out in the rain with the rest of your people," Vermeulen said. He shook it off like *he* had been the one insulted and continued, "The doors will be locked for the night. It's just too dangerous with some mystery killer monster out there to leave it open."

"I don't think it can work a doorknob," I said.

"No, but the miners can. And they will no longer have access to this building."

"*What*?" Ellie cried. "What if there's another attack out there?"

Vermeulen looked a little green at the prospect. He tugged at his cuffs and said, "It is the decision of my board of directors. It's not me—I don't want anything bad to happen to the miners—"

"Even if they *are* Negroes," Atari spat.

The company man stiffened at that. "This discussion is over. The doors will be bolted at sundown. If you are inside at that time, you may stay comfortably. If not, then you throw in your lot with the Congolese."

"What a good German," Gregory said, and Daan Vermeulen actually flinched. "Follow those orders no matter what, eh?"

Vermeulen turned on his heel—with ironic military precision—and stomped away into the depths of the building. He slammed a door, making his office workers jump.

"It's noon," I said. "Can you guys stomach eating with these people before we go off in search of the Jeep?"

"I'd rather go hungry," Atari said, making us smile unfairly, but then he reached into his poncho and brought out some thousand-calories energy bars. "But we don't have to."

***

"How long can it *rain* like this?" Ellie yelled, as she had to do for us to hear anyone else in the still-gushing downpour.

"It's the rainforest," I shouted back. "The *African* rainforest. There's a distinct possibility it will *never* stop."

She smiled at that, and I was glad. "Wish we had Bonte and his car right now!"

"No, he'd go too fast," Atari said loudly, his eyes glued to the infrared monitor on the specialized camera. "We only got about 20 feet visibility as it is. We could be in a ditch or run right into a tree faster than I could say *stop*."

We had moved out of the Vermeulen building and made our way to the guard station, both of the men inside staying warm and dry as they waved to us in ironic pity. Assholes.

Now Atari led us to the gate, and then we apparently were out in the open area with the armored car—yes, that's just where we were, and Atari used that to navigate with the infrared camera in the direction we hoped to hell we had left the destroyed Jeep.

"There it is!" our cameraman yelled joyfully, and we all peered in at the monitors. It was visible, as had been most of our other metal markers like gateposts and the armored car as a black, cold area in the screen mostly brightened by the warm rain. "I can't believe it's still there!"

"Don't get too excited," I said. "They probably came and stripped the M40 off it already."

"You didn't mention that as a possibility," Gregory said, not exactly mad but not exactly happy, either.

I wanted to say that one would have to assume this was the case, but then I thought back to my devastating conversation with the Boss. You can't assume that you know the truth every time. So I didn't respond, just kept walking in our little troupe's shuffling steps toward the Jeep on Atari's infrared camera. As we got within ten steps, the screen changed and glowed from trees and standing water, not from the torrents of rain.

Because, as abruptly as it had begun, the deluge stopped.

The Jeep was right there, burnt and blackened and broken.

Its machine gun was gone.

Before we even had time to lament our rotten luck, three Jeeps—each with a big ol' M40 mounted in front—surrounded us. And who hopped out of one of them but Captain Jeep himself? He spoke in French, making sure I understood every foreign word. "We knew you would come back," he said, and grabbed Atari's camera and dashed it against the ground. Then he went and stood right in front of Ellie. "And you didn't think I would forget *you*, did you, lovely lady?"

As casually as possible, I reached for my pistols—they were more like clothing to me and I was just as likely to neglect to put them on when going outside—but cold steel touched the back of my neck and I stopped. My guns were lifted from me, and the militia soldiers checked Atari and Gregory for weapons as well. They had none, since a legitimate camera crew wouldn't.

"Hold her arms back for me, would you, Brett Russell?"

I started. "How do you know—"

Captain Jeep slapped Ellie hard, right across the face. She yelped in pain but stood defiant. "Hold her *arms* for me, *would you, Brett Russell?*" he repeated through clenched yellow teeth.

This time I stepped over to Ellie and loosely held her wrists behind her. "I'm sorry," I whispered to her.

She started a reply but was cut short as the captain kicked his thick, hard boot right into Ellie's crotch, against her pelvis and probably her whole ... *area* down there. She doubled over in pain, and Cappy took advantage of her position to bring a knee up to her forehead. She went straight into the mud, her eyes slightly open in her unconsciousness.

Captain Jeep said something in Swahili or Kikongo, and the men responded by tossing the redhead into the back of his vehicle. "Remember my men, Brett Russell? This is called 'the paying back.'" He then pulled a .45 automatic out of his holster and shot Gregory through the head. The big man was dead before his body hit the ground.

He shifted to point it at Atari's face. The younger man shut his eyes, calmly awaiting his death. (Maybe meditation worked.) There was nothing I could do to save him, either, the soldier's gun still against my neck. I'd never be able to swing around in time to grab the gun before he pulled the trigger.

"*Comment tu t'appelles?*" he said to Atari as he pushed the barrel of his .45 against Atari's right eye socket.

"W-What?"

Captain Jeep slapped Atari's cheek and repeated his question: "*Comment tu t'appelles?*"

"I don't speak Fr—"

"He wants to know your name," I said, wondering what the Captain's game was but also not wanting to find out.

"Atari," the cameraman said, shaking.

"Well, Monsieur Atari," Cappy said in English, the son of a bitch, "you live for now. Go tell your boss at the mines that we are taking what is ours very soon. No more miners come to work for him. *Go!*" He punctuated his sentence with the butt of his gun against Atari's forehead, creating a gash that immediately poured blood down his face.

"*Jesus*, man!" Atari looked shocked in addition to physically injured.

"No Jesus for you—*sors d'ici!*" Cap practically screamed in our cameraman's face. Atari scrambled to run away and out of view toward the Vermeulen camp. out of the room and out the door.

"Now, Brett Russell, you come answer some questions before I kill you, okay?" he said brightly and motioned to his men to stuff me in the back seat of another Jeep while the captain drove off in the vehicle containing an unconscious Ellie White.

# CHAPTER 13

This was not ideal. Ellie was tied to a wooden chair next to me, easy to do when she was unconscious, and I was tied to a chair, easy to do when you had a loaded gun pressed against my temple. This all seemed a bit Saturday Republic Serial to me, but it wasn't exciting. Just nerve-wracking. Also, my anger over Captain Jeep's murder of Gregory the sound man was threatening to boil over and make me take some impulsive, useless actions that would do wonders for relieving stress but just about nothing to keep Ellie and me alive.

"I am General Cephu," the man I had formerly called Captain said to me in English after he let off a little steam by punching me in the face a couple of times, breaking my nose but not my desire to kill him.

"General, huh?" I said in English, spitting blood. "I should've figured. General Confusion, maybe, or General Failure."

"Your idiot words mean nothing to me," he said in English, which I expected, since I was sticking to colloquial language this asshole would *almost*, but not quite, understand. He puffed out his chest, literally. "You killed three of my soldiers, three men faithful to the rebellion we are inciting."

"Listen, Princess Leia, I don't have a dog in your fight. I don't give two shits about your rebellion. All I know is you were set to snuff my new BFF."

Cephu's face scrunched; he probably thought his English was superior, just like he thought everything else about himself was superior. "*What?*" he said in amusing frustration.

"I *said* that I couldn't give a rat's ass about *why* you're kicking people's buckets for them, just that your sidekicks earned getting their tickets punched for putting a pea-shooter to Atari's noggin, *capisce?*"

The general chambered a round and placed the muzzle of his .45 right against my kneecap. He said, "I certainly hope I can understand you this time, Mister Russell."

I took it Cephu wasn't in a funnin' mood. I cleared my throat and said, "I killed your men because they were going to kill my friend and then possibly me. I would have killed you, too, if you weren't in a position where you could hurt the girl before I got you. I am not interested in your rebellion."

He took the gun off my knee, and I let out a nervous breath I didn't even realize I was holding. "You work for Vermeulen."

"I do not. I am here with the television show *Cryptids Alive!*"

"Then why does Vermeulen Mining give you food and shelter? They do not make television programs." Cephu seemed to think he had the upper hand not only physically, but also logically, maybe morally. "I am told you are not a television man, that you are here instead to infiltrate my militia."

Despite my tan from being outside a lot, I was still blindingly light-skinned compared to the almost purple blackness of the general's skin. "That sounds ... difficult."

Cephu laughed, and I smiled with him for protective reasons. "Here is what I want: you will leave Tshikapa tomorrow and never come back, you and what's left of the television crew. We have Vermeulen right exactly where we want them, and an American spy working for them isn't going to ruin that."

"General Amusement—"

"Cephu!"

"*Gesundheit.* Anyway, I accede to your demands. I will leave here along with Ellie"—I nodded at the slowly waking woman—"and Atari and the sound man you killed. We'll pack into planes at get out of here."

"I am not making jokes here, Mister Russell."

"Neither am I. We are out of here ... based on one condition: You answer a question for me."

"Wass ... wass goin on?" Ellie murmured as she opened her eyes and straightened her neck and back to sit up. She saw me tied up and Cephu with his semi-automatic pistol and said, "Aw, *shit.*"

Cephu threw his head back and laughed. "She understands the trouble you are in, Mister Russell. She is not making demands." He called out to two of his compatriots who must have been standing just outside the doorway. "Dany, Salomon, what do you think of this beautiful white lady?"

They spoke in Swahili to Cephu, then the general to them. Sickening smiles adorned all of their faces as they leered at Ellie, who now looked more nervous than pissed off.

"She didn't do anything, General. Let her go."

He whacked me across the forehead with the butt of his gun, just as he had done with Atari. And just like Atari, blood streamed down my face. "You make so many *demands*, American. You make demands and I give you choices."

"Choices?" I didn't like the sound of that.

"Yes, indeed, sir. Dany and Salomon are very good soldiers who deserve some of the spoils of war," he said, again looking over at Ellie tied to her chair. "But whether they get them, that is up to you, Mister Russell."

"What's my choice? You kill her first or you kill me first?"

Cephu translated to his two henchmen, and they all laughed. Such a great time everyone was having! "No, no, no. You live for now. Your choice is about Miss White—would you like me to kill her right now, or allow Dany and Salomon their reward and let them rape her. Then, after that, I kill her."

All the color drained from Ellie's face. I could see her hands trying to work the knot, but she wasn't going to be able to untie it. I had been Special Forces and I couldn't untie a knot tied in a rope of that thickness without being able to see what I was doing. I know, because I had been trying since they bound me to my chair.

I know I could execute a Black Widow kind of move, doing a front flip and crashing the chair against the floor to splinter into a thousand pieces, then jump and bring my arms in front of me, where I could then subdue the militia general and his soldiers, untie my hands and then Ellie's and make a run for it.

However.

Chair *legs* might break off with such a superhero maneuver, but it was unlikely a real wooden chair of any solidity would explode into shards and allow me freedom. Also unlike in the movies, three armed men would be unlikely to just stand there and gawk as I beat each of them to a pulp with my bound hands, etc., etc. They had powerful guns and they would use them on me at point-blank range, killing me. And then they would rape and kill my sweet, charming, ball-busting Ellie White.

*My?* I meant *the*. The Ellie White, not *my* Ellie White. LOL, as the kids like to say.

"What is your choice, Mister Spy?"

Ellie looked absolutely petrified now, and I couldn't say I blamed her. Still, I had to use the only ploy I could, which was stalling the soldiers until I could think of a better ploy. So I said, "I won't make a choice until you answer my question."

The general laughed most heartily once again, and Dany and Salomon followed suit even though they had no idea what I had just said. "Do you really think you're getting out of here alive? Her, you, the fat boy, any of you?"

"Doesn't matter. Just answer me one question."

"All right, James Bonds, ask your question."

There are bluffs and then there are seat-of-your pants, I-hope-to-God-I-sound-even slightly-convincing, shot-in-the-dark uneducated *guesses*. What I did was completely and utterly the latter. I straightened in my chair, thrust out my chin a little bit, giving Cephu a little show of incredibly confident body language, and said: "What are your men doing in the jungle in the middle of the night to make that Kasai Rex attack the miners?"

The generals' face turned from smug and smarmy to open-mouthed shock in less than one second. Then he laughed, maybe out of surprise, maybe out of genuine amusement. "How in the ancestor's holy names do you know this?" he said when he could talk again, then explained to his two soldiers. Their mouths dropped open then, too, and they didn't recover their composure by laughing.

I couldn't believe I had nailed it on the head, but then, who else could it have been?

"I am going to tell you, Mister Russell. Maybe you believe it, maybe you don't. But I tell you the truth because who cares? You will be dead soon, after you finish watching us rape and kill your girlfriend."

"Hey! What happened to me making the choice?"

Cephu guffawed again. "We were going to do it anyway. So do you want to hear the truth or should my boys just begin?"

*Stall, stall, stall.* And I had to *think*, for God's sake.

The general couldn't keep his hilarity to himself, so he shared his evil comment to Dany and Salomon, making them laugh for real. The one I thought was Dany leaned into Cephu and said something which even in Swahili sounded filthy as hell, and both men laughed again.

"What's Tweedledum got to say?" I asked, trying not to care, but needing to know for my own sanity. I had absolutely nothing to even make these criminals pause, and I think my stalling by talking was falling to the law of decreasing returns.

"Salomon says she is the whitest woman he had ever seen, but he's going to burn her to black with his fiery *uume*. That means his penis."

"Yeah, I figured," I said, but "burning" made me think of the cheroot in my front pocket and the *book of matches* in my back pocket. "S-So tell me this big secret, already." It was hard to keep control of my breath and not look like I was squirming around suspiciously as I lifted the book out. All I had to do was drop it and we were both dead, with Ellie wishing she were dead before they actually killed her.

I didn't drop it.

"Okay, I break the suspense now. What are we doing in the dark jungle to make the monster kill the mine people? We steal her *egg*, stupid man. We steal it and run away before she can catch us."

Despite her predicament, Ellie perked up. "There are *eggs*? That means there's more than one! She must have a mate! And the eggs—maybe they're not the first! Brett, there could be a whole extended family of Kasai Rex in that jungle!"

Salomon—no, Dany—stepped forward and slapped her hard across the face. Tears came to her eyes and she shut up, but there was no mistaking that the cryptid hunter was still excited.

"You steal the monster's *eggs*?" I said, not getting it. "Why does that make the Kasai Rex kill the miners?"

"Ha! I can tell you have never had a child."

My eye twitched. It suddenly became much easier to fish out one of the matches, which I could strike against the wood of the chair as soon as General Cephu looked away.

But that was not going to happen yet. "The mother, she can smell that people like us—what do you Americans call us?"

"Black people."

"That is not it!" he said, and laughed again. "We both know what it is. She can smell that *niggers* have taken her precious baby, and she comes running for it. We leave it as far into the tents as can and then run like the devil himself."

"How did you even know there was a Kasai Rex in that jungle? It's never even been mapped out! *Scientists* don't even know about it!"

"Never mind that, Mister Spy. We leave the eggs by the tents and then Mother comes to find it, totally in rage and killing anything she sees until she finds it again and takes it back to the nest. It kills the dumb miners again and again and still they won't refuse to work for Vermeulen. Still they won't join us! What stupid and ridiculous people they are!"

Ellie looked even more excited at the thought of a *nest* of cryptids, but the reddening welt on her cheek was doing its job of keeping her silent for now.

"They probably know you'll treat them even worse than the Belgians. You'll make them from virtual slaves into *actual* slaves."

"Ha! Who cares! They'll still be alive, won't they? Where is the gratitude for us saving them from the monsters?" Seeing the disgust on my face, Cephu laughed again. "And besides, once Vermeulen is gone, the price of diamonds goes way up for the miners—or for those who are in charge and their soldiers, anyway—because we shall have an automatic buyer, no middle man!"

"I can tell you want me to ask who this buyer is," I said. My fingers were poised to strike the match. "So, okay, who's the buyer?"

"*I don't know!*" he yelled in my face with delight. "But he tell us he got control over so many of the mines here, billions for them by the time the shiny rocks go to your malls and supermarkets!"

"This big company, they finance you assholes?"

"Not yet, but it all comes when we get control of this mine! Shiny cars, lots of guns, we will get everything your money can buy! We make all the money in the world, live like American rappers! Bling, bling! *Ha ha ha!*"

"What's the company, goddamnit?"

"They don't tell us, stupid! To us, they just give money and tell us how to get richer than rich! We just call them *shirika*."

"What's that in English?" I asked, dreading the answer.

"I don't know it in English."

"French, then! *Tell me!*"

The general thought for a moment, then said, "Em, in French would be *l'organisation*."

I squeezed my eyes shut. I must have been going insane. The Organization—*my* Organization—was the number-one *killer* of endangered animals? *And* they killed my family to keep me loyal? *And* now it was behind the killing of these miners, hundreds of innocent people, *and* it had almost total control over the Congolese diamond mining industry?

This all didn't make an iota of sense. And it was awfully goddamn *convenient*. I couldn't make any of it line up. In my twelve years with The Organization, there had never been a shred of evidence it was anything but the benefactor to the world that I thought it was. "The Organization," I said at last.

Cephu smiled in surprise. "*Oh!* It is the same name in English!"

I just couldn't think of any of this for one more second. I just had to get us out—myself and Ellie. God, Ellie. I had told her everything and she had told *them*. But she gave them my secrets—*them*, the bastards who had just killed her loyal sound man—by acting like she cared about me, and at just the right moment. "I got my answer. Now rape her and kill her, go for it. I want to see it."

"*Brett!*" she screamed, very convincingly.

Cephu's yellow grin was matched as soon as he translated what I had said to his two compatriots. The three men laughed heartily and started removing their clothing for a nice long rape … which was not what I was expecting to happen. They were supposed to *pause*, because it was all a bluff on their part, right? They weren't going to kill the mole if they were going to kill me anyway. *Right?*

*Oh, hell.*

I had made an epic miscalculation.

I mouthed "My bad! Hold on!" to Ellie and, seeing the men in various states of undress, struck the match against my chair and held it to the thick rope. It started smoking almost immediately, then burning in a matter of seconds. The men remained focused on getting naked to rape Ellie, and the low flame eating away the rope was so near my bound hands I thought I would start screaming from the pain. Fortunately for me, I was able to shift in my chair enough to maneuver the burning part of the knot on top, so the heat rose away from my tender hands.

It was a race now. The burning through the ropes versus the soldiers finishing getting their boots off and getting to work on Ellie. I couldn't see the burning, but my hands felt looser in the unwinding fibers.

However, they were all naked now, their cocks ready for Ellie's creamy skin. Not paying me the slightest attention now, they yanked down her khakis, not even bothering to get her boots off first. Her legs shook as she struggled against them trying to remove her panties.

*Almost there. Come on* ... My hands felt like they were on fire, and maybe they were. But it didn't matter—I was able at last to break through the charred remains of the rope binding me and in one motion pulled my hands apart and in front of me, jumping up out of the chair as I did so. I shouted "Ellie!"—as if she couldn't see me get up from the chair and shake off the smoldering rope—and, her boots never removed by her would-be rapists and her khakis acting as binding to keep her ankles together, she swung up both her feet and smashed General Cephu right in what I could see was his remaining testicle. She used the tread of her boots and raked it up and down his crotch. When she finished, it was no longer there.

He howled and fell to the floor and I got to the soldiers' discarded uniforms before they could even turn away from their victim. I found one of their .45s almost instantly and put bullets in the both their heads. As they fell, I realized why I couldn't tell Davy from Salomon—they were twins, down to the matching birthmarks on their chests. So a family reunion, I guess.

I undid Ellie's bonds—easy enough when you could see what you were doing—and held her close with my blistered wrists. "I thought you told them my … what I shared with you back in the tent," I said, almost ready to cry again. "I'm sorry."

She breathed out a laugh that was also a sigh of relief. "When would I have done that? On the drive over here? I was *unconscious*, you meathead!"

She said with a forgiving smile, but I had to say, "But how could they know anything about The Organization? Unless …"

"Unless they're working with the militia to take control of the mine," she said, putting her clothes back on, and frowned at my expression. "Hey! I *am* a journalist, you know!"

"Great," I said, ignoring the pain in my wrists as I grabbed the semi-conscious and all-castrated General Cephu and forced his pants up and belted them. He had no shirt on, but we weren't going to a fancy restaurant. "How about you interview this witness?"

# CHAPTER 14

Every dip in the ground was filled with water, and it still dripped rain from the trees, but the sky was blue like the hours-long storm had never happened. I kept hold of Cephu by his belt and marched him to one of the Jeeps, keys in the ignition. His khakis were drenched in crotch blood, but it was drying now, so the bleeding must have stopped. I sat him in the shotgun seat and helped Ellie into the back seat. I gave her one of our now-plentiful handguns and said, "He makes a move, shoot him in the spine. He won't die, but he'll be a beggar on the street the rest of his life."

I had no reason to think the general understood every English word I said, but I could tell by his slow but insistent shaking of his head that he didn't want such a fate. That was fine by me—I needed him for just one thing and then he could go live his eunuch's life for all it was worth.

"I want you to take me to our cameraman. And you'd *better* pray he's alive and well."

His eyes opened. "Your cameraman? I don't know who—"

I slapped him upside the head and said, "Our *friend*. The black kid. Atari. The one you were going to *kill*, remember?"

Despite everything, his mouth opened in a smile. "From when you blow up my Jeep and kill my men?"

"And I ripped one of your balls off," Ellie chimed in from the back.

"He is your *friend*?" Cephu said and couldn't keep himself from laughing. "Yes, I take you right to him!"

"Well, all right," I said, and started the Jeep.

Cephu led us directly to the front door of the Vermeulen Mining concrete bunker. "This is the place, *mons amis*. Now take me inside to the clinic?"

I slapped myself in the forehead. Of *course* this was where Atari was—was he not ordered to go tell Vermeulen that very soon he wouldn't have any more miners to abuse? Of course, even the casually racist Daan Vermeulen wouldn't throw Atari out when the militia is killing people. He wasn't white, but he was American, and that counted for a lot in this oddball end of the world.

"Take me to the clinic now, yes?"

"No. We can grab you some peroxide on our way out."

I had stuck Ellie's rope into my front pocket—the one without my two remaining cheroots in it—and now I tied the general's hands through the steering wheel in a knot he would need three hands to get out of. "You watch the car. We'll be right back."

His face and voice couldn't decide if he was petrified or highly amused as he shouted, "You go in there, you not *ever* coming back!"

This put a chill in our spines, but Ellie and I didn't know what else to do except rescue Atari—if he even needed rescuing; he could be asleep on a feather bed in a guest room for all we know. Cephu's laughing, terrified warning made us, after being buzzed in, enter the Vermeulen building with a trepidation neither of us had felt even a moment before.

\*\*\*

As we entered, a shrill fire alarm pounded our arms, and blinking safety LEDs added to the atmosphere of impending disaster. But there was no smoke, no screaming or even mildly inconvenienced workers making a move to leave through the door we had just entered from, the only one we were aware of. (Congolese safety codes were as foldable as a handful of cash.)

We walked down the carpeted hallway as before, but the left-hand side, the one that had provided a safe space for the miners and their families during the Kasai Rex attack, was no longer besmirched with even a spot of mud. It was shiny and clean—and empty.

"Better this than housing dirty workers," I muttered to Ellie as we moved toward Vermeulen's vault-like office farther back, the sirens still blaring, the lights still flashing.

She looked over to the office section on the right and said, "Where did everyone go?"

I stopped, and she did as well. I stared through the glass and saw monitors left on, screensavers on some, spreadsheets or Web pages still open on others. Every office chair was pushed in, however, and there was no untidiness anywhere we could see.

"Who buzzed us in if everybody's gone?" Ellie asked.

I leaned in through a door to the office section and called out, "Hello? Anybody here?" I assumed the Vermeulen workers spoke English because ... well, I'm an American.

As soon as I had finished my call, however, the sound and light show stopped. At that, the workers who had stuffed themselves into each office against the wall, plus a copy room, closets, and a kitchen—all areas with doors that closed—streamed out of their safe places and returned to their workstations, chatting as if nothing had happened. Because, apparently, nothing had.

"Um, hello?" Ellie said to a young woman coming our way but who just about jumped out of her skin when she saw us.

Then she laughed and said, "*Je maakte me bang!*"

Ellie smiled along with her but added sheepishly, "English?"

"Ah! You scared me!" She seemed friendly and not frightened by anything other than us popping into the doorway while she wasn't looking.

"What's going on?" I asked, following Ellie into the office proper. "What were you all hiding from?"

"I think maybe it was a surprise drill?" she said, looking unperturbed. "When we get a Code Black siren, it means there is maybe a crazy gun-shooter in the building, you know? The doors aren't bulletproof, but we hope security comes before the shooting person finds us, you see?"

We did, indeed. "Where's security, then?"

"It maybe was just a drill, like I say. Security doesn't really have to come and rescue us, you know?"

"Of course," I said, but something was definitely not right. "We need to see Mister Vermeulen, please."

"I believe he was in a meeting when the Code Black went off."

"Mind if we check?" I asked, already herding Ellie and myself out the door so that any resistance would be more or less futile. "It's rather important."

"I'll ring him, wait just a moment, okay?" she said, and picked up a receiver and punched a single button. "Oh, hello! Mister Vermeulen has two guests, please. Yes, they ..." she trailed off, then looked at the receiver funny and hung it up.

"All good?" Ellie said.

"Yes, all good," she said, not looking like all was good, but whatever, we had business to tend to. Like finding out what the hell had happened to Atari? *Had* there been a gunman in the building, but one with a specific American, chubby, black target?

We made haste to Vermeulen's office and rapped at the heavy door.

"Come in," Atari called from the other side.

\*\*\*

The replacement *Cryptids Alive!* cameraman sat in the plush chair behind Vermeulen's desk, with the executive himself seated in one of the also-nice chairs facing the desk.

"Hello, guys! Have a seat," Atari said brightly, the wound on his forehead stitched and bandaged. He was also wearing a new button-down shirt, one that fit him much better than the *Star Wars* and *Doctor Who* tees he wore when he was with the rest of us. Maybe Vermeulen lent him one to make up for his ... racist ... bullsh ...

Daan Vermeulen was dead. A bullet hole marred his gray suit jacket right over where his heart would have been. He sat in the chair exactly as if he had been alive, no stiffness setting in yet.

Meaning he had been shot quite recently. I guessed it was about the time of the Code Black that sent everyone scurrying into closets and boardrooms. I could also guess that the missing security guards had been compensated well enough not to make a big deal out of the whole thing.

But by who? *Atari?*

"Have a seat, I said," Atari repeated, all smile gone from his face. "Sit on his lap if you don't want to touch a dead man, Ellie. You'll be around another soon enough, anyway."

"What the *hell* is going on, Atari?" Ellie snapped, not thrown by his weird demeanor and threatening words. "You *killed* Vermeulen? You're *killing* people now? What happened to 'I'm a Buddhist, I don't like killing—"

"Sit *down!*" he shouted, and suddenly he looked less like a young and chubby audiovisual enthusiast and more like a bloated mobster holding every ace in the deck.

I sat down in the open chair and Ellie sat on my knee. Not my lap, but Atari had been close enough. Even if we were willing to move the body, it didn't look like the luckiest seat in the house anyway. "We're sitting," I said. "Now please tell us what in the hell is going on." I was surprised that my own voice didn't sound more angry, but this day had just about used up every ounce of anger my system could produce.

Or so I thought. "First of all," he said, "my name isn't *Atari*. It isn't Nintendo or Xbox, either, smartmouth, before you try to get all hilarious on me."

A jibe of that nature had occurred to me, but luckily he hadn't given me a chance to deliver it.

"Second, I just killed this son of a bitch twenty minutes ago, tops. I came in here and delivered my message from Cephu and the boys—Salomon didn't have to hit me that hard, *shit*. Old Daan here wasn't terribly impressed. In fact, he told me he didn't need a gang of tree-swingers telling him what to do with his company. That didn't make me feel well-disposed toward him, I admit."

"So you shot him," Ellie said.

"Who's telling this story, you dumb whore?"

"*Whoa, whoa*, Atari! That's going too—"

He jumped up out of the cushy chair and yelled, "*My name ain't Atari, asshole!*"

He was holding quite the hand-cannon. I believe if we moved Daan Vermeulen, we would find a .357 slug had gone right through him, the back of the chair, and well into the thick wall. My hands went up automatically—I was almost getting used to people sticking guns in my face—and I felt Ellie freeze on my knee. Should I say something? Or would that just set off not-Atari? I calmed my breath and asked, "Then what *is* your name?"

The person who I am going to continue to refer to as "Atari" smiled ruefully, and the gun went a little slack in his hands, so we weren't dead yet. "You really don't recognize me, do you?"

Ellie and I looked at each other, then back at our host. "Me?" Ellie said.

"No, I mean Mister Commando, Mister Number-One Operative."

*What the shit?* "I was in the Special Forces, if that's what you mean."

"No, I mean your job since then. What we call 'The Organization.' Ring a bell?"

Did *everyone* know about this top-secret entity and my role in it now? I played dumb, but half-heartedly. He obviously knew whatever he knew, and that obviously included who I was and what I did. "You're right," I said. "I *don't* recognize you."

"Yeah, I thought not. Nobody pays attention to the IT guy, the underpaid, overworked son of a bitch who has access to your emails going back and forth to ——————," he said, giving a name to the person I only know as the Boss. "Plane tickets, weapons purchases, it's all there. The Organization—by the way, its name is"—here he gave an actual name to our shadowy employer, nothing I had ever heard before—"is breaking so many international laws and treaties at once, I could bring the whole house of cards down with one well-placed phone call."

I'm an asshole, okay? So I couldn't stop myself, and even if I could have, I wouldn't have: I said, "Is this monologuing? Are you a villain? We get to hear your whole evil plan now, right?"

Atari raised his .357 magnum again and pointed it at Ellie. "One more comment like that and she gets it in the breadbasket, all right? She'll go septic and die before you can even get her into sorry excuse for a hospital."

"All right, all right, sorry," I said, and I could feel a trickle of sweat go down my face. "So you're a disgruntled Organization IT manager, and now you're getting revenge on them by … killing miners? I actually wouldn't mind a monologue, because I have no goddamned idea what is going on."

He lowered the gun again. "Look at me. Look at my face. I've talked to you like a dozen times in the *one* year I've been at [The Organization]. You don't recognize me at *all*."

"I don't. But all of you people look alike to me; I don't bother differentiating between you."

Ellie and Atari both yelped, "*What?*"

"Not *black* people, for Chrissakes. The other *employees*, the cubicle gophers. I assiduously avoid any contact with them. I'm in the field most of the time, so it doesn't matter to me who they are. And I don't want to become a security leak by knowing other people's business at The Organization."

"And despite all that, now you're the spy left out in the cold. Right, isn't that what [The Boss] said? Now that you know they killed your family, now that you believe in cryptids, now that you know what [The Organization] does with the animals you 'rescue,' you know too much. Isn't that pretty much the gist of it?"

In a day of shocks, this one was one that left me speechless ... for a moment. I found my voice and said as I pushed Ellie to her feet and stood in front of the dead man's desk, "There is no way you could know that, any of it. It was a secure line and the storm forced us to go to text mode. You couldn't have overheard what I said, because I didn't *say* it at all—it was *text*."

"This is the part of the monologuing where I blow your mind. Ready?"

"I doubt it."

"Ha! That was me on the sat-phone. I wasn't meditating or doing whatever faggoty thing you all thought in that tent room of mine. I hijacked the signal with my equipment—all you need is a factory-made laptop with the right software and a little extra hardware—and texted to you whatever I could think of to break you, make you give up and go away. When that didn't work, I sent Cephu and his boys to kill you, which they apparently couldn't do because they're goddamn *apes*. I hate Africa. It makes me feel like I'm at a family reunion attended only by violent retards."

I squinted at him. "That was *not* you on the sat-phone. That was my Boss's voice and rhythm, even if it was just text. We've sent automatically erasing emails a million times, and this exactly matched his cadences and words he'd use. No, you're bluffing, trying to make me doubt everything all over again."

Atari put the monster handgun on the desk—a good sign, but one I hardly registered at the moment, so turned around was I. "It's a very minor tweak in Linux to make your emails 'automatically erase' themselves from your computer and [The Boss]'s as well," he said, "while keeping everything archived for myself. It was trivial then to construct a bot that would automatically make suggestions on how to write in 'Boss-speak.' I just approximate the best I can, but the bot makes it match his ... what did you call it? His *cadence*, his *rhythm*? His word choices? The point is, I'm a goddamn genius and you are a goddamn trusting idiot."

"Congratulations. If what you're saying is true, then the Boss doesn't know anything about what's going on here?"

"I prefer to play that one close to the chest," Atari said, and I couldn't help but see his man-boobs making his nice shirt strain a little at the front. He stood up and stuck the .357 in the waistband in the back of his slacks. "What 'The Organization' doesn't know won't hurt me."

Ellie and I looked at each other. Were we supposed to stand, too? What was the protocol for not pissing off an armed villain? I shook the thought out of my head—there were no villains. There were only people with a different conception of "good"—maybe a completely insane conception à la Adolf and the Boys, but their conception nonetheless. So what was Atari getting out of all this Machiavellian subterfuge? He said he was "overworked and underpaid" as an IT guy at our employer—did he do it for the money that would come as a result of the diamond mine? Was this revenge for some imagined snub by me back at headquarters when he upgraded my computer? Did he hate Congo and its inhabitants for some reason, or the Belgians? I was at a loss.

"Stand up." Okay, one question answered. We stood. Atari pressed the intercom button on his desk phone and said, "Melanie, get Bonte to base. Tell him to bring the boat."

"For the fresh meat?" an office worker's voice sounded from the speaker and laughed.

Atari laughed, too. "Don't you guys worry about it—just get the office pool together and we'll see who dies first, and how."

"Where are we going?" Ellie blurted immediately.

"*We* ain't going nowhere, not unless you got a mouse in your pocket. You and Indiana Jackass here are gonna get the chance to do what you came here for—you'll get your story and he'll get a chance to save an endangered species. That is," he said to me, "if you can save your own dumb asses first."

I had no power to stop him, but I blocked his way around the desk anyway and said, "It's not monologuing until you tell us *why*. Why in the hell are you doing this?"

Atari laughed heartily, a much deeper and angrier laugh than he had ever given when he was in his cameraman persona. "You mean, other than getting rid of these lazy Negro miners and getting some modern equipment up in here to get those diamonds up out the ground?"

"*Lazy?*" Ellie protested, unable to control herself. "They work 16 hours a d—"

"Yeah, yeah, whatever. Now they won't have to do—Ima turn those diamonds around myself and make a shitload—*a* shit*load*— of money."

"So you're doing all this for money."

"No, little lady," Atari said as if I weren't there, "there are *so* many other reasons. [The Organization] didn't want an asthmatic butterball like me in the field, saving animals. I *love* animals, but no—ain't gonna have no *colored boy* going out and catching poachers."

"So revenge on [The Organization]?"

"Ellie, *listen*. There's no bottom to the well of why I'm doing this. Taking care of this next batch of miners is just what this company needs to go onto the chopping block at a pennies-on-the-dollar discount. The hostile takeover—if you can even call it that—doesn't even need to be *hostile* anymore, since the unfortunate death of Mister Vermeulen there. It's business mixed with pleasure. I would think you'd get that, a creamy white Harvard-educated—"

"Vassar, actually."

*Ha! I knew it!* You can't mistake a Vassar—

"—educated *bitch*, running around chasing Bigfoot and Sasquatch—"

"Those are the same cryp—"

"*I know that!* Now shut up before I kill you right here and don't let you see the Kasai Rex yourself!"

I could feel myself turn three shades of green. "Seeing" the Kasai Rex meant going into the jungle again, that uncharted jungle full of monsters. Atari's little army obviously knew where to find the nest and could find their way back out. But Ellie and me …

A polite knock came at the door.

"Melanie?" Atari called.

The door opened and a little white face bearing a wicked smirk poked in. "Bonte is here, sir," she said in a slimy European accent, then paused to give Ellie and myself a disgusted look. "For the cargo."

Atari laughed and motioned for us to lead the way, with him at the rear once he had picked up his hand-cannon again and stuck it in my back. We shuffled out of the office, following Melanie, who drew the attention of the office workers behind the glass, most of whom—no, wait, *all* of whom—were sniggering at the coming fate of the stupid Americans.

I shot them the bird. I don't know if that's something they have in Belgium, but they were welcome to it. I had a lot more to give.

Melanie got to the front door (the only door, as far as I could still tell) and held it open as Atari marched us to our doom. Outside, with General Cephu's knotted rope exchanged for handcuffs that shackled him to the oar holder of a small motorboat dragged behind his station wagon, was an abjectly miserable-looking Bonte.

Looking past him, I could see the miners all hard at it, slipping in and out of holes, digging at the sides of shallower pits, easily a hundred people including the women and children, maybe more.

Atari was going to kill every one of them to get control of this mine.

*This* mine.

I stopped, even as Atari jabbed me with the revolver. "There's one more question I have to ask you, even though you've danced around every other."

"Okay, Scout's honor, I'll give you a straight answer, I totes promise," Atari mocked.

"There are hundreds of diamond mines in Congo. Why this one?"

Atari pulled on my shoulder to turn me around to face him. "Because this place has a pre-installed monster, and *something* was dragging off an occasional animal or child ... and adult, actually. The call to *Cryptids Alive!* and also to [The Organization] originated from Tshikapa, and that meant our employer would be sending their number-one operative: *You.*

"You, Brett Russell, wonderboy poacher hunter, would get every ounce of blame for things going FUBAR here. And I would clean up to get every penny. It was the perfect situation, one I had been waiting for this entire past year."

"Did you tell me the truth about The Organization using operatives to provide them with endangered animals for private hunting?"

"You said you had one question, you got one answer. Now get in the goddamn car—you both got an appointment with fate."

I didn't move. "What about my family? Were they who really killed my family?"

Atari pointed his gun right at Ellie's chest and said, "Any more questions? How about one bullet in the bitch for 'no,' two for 'yes'?"

I shut my eyes, shut my mouth. We climbed into the station wagon's back seat, General Cephu cuffed in the shotgun seat, looking sick as shit. I didn't have to wonder why—his balls had been ripped off and he had lost a lot of blood. If he didn't get some antibiotics and some of the red stuff fairly soon, his end was going to be long and extremely unpleasant. *Much* better was how Ellie and I were about to die, swallowed whole by a mythical creature.

"General Cephu," Atari called to the semi-conscious figure in English, "catch," and tossed him one of the militia's .45s. "Show these fine people where your boys get the eggs, and we'll get you all fixed up, 'kay? *Do NOT shoot them* unless they refuse to follow orders."

Cephu picked up the weapon, and I could only imagine how much he wanted to put a bullet into each of our brains right then.

"Cephu!" Atari barked. "You understand me? I want *them* bringing the eggs back. *They're* gonna have the fun of killing the miners this time."

The general kept his wavering gaze at the .45 in his lap, but mustered a nod.

"Excellent."

Bonte got into the driver's seat and shut his door. Atari leaned in close to him and spoke low into his ear. Whatever he said, it made Bonte nod solemnly and start the car.

"Goodbye!" Atari yelled with a cheery tone as Bonte dragged us and the boat down to the river. "You assholes keep it warm in Hell for me, ya hear?"

# CHAPTER 15

"Bonte, man, stop the car. We'll get out and run," I said.

But the smiling, jovial Bonte we had met earlier had vanished. In his place was a gray-looking simulacrum who barely had a voice to answer me with: "Monsieur Bushnell says they have my family under guard up in the village."

"Monsieur Bushnell?"

"The bad man. The one who came with you." *Atari*, he meant.

Ellie said, "'Under guard'—isn't that a good thing?"

Bonte shook his head mournfully. "They are not keeping anyone out. They are keeping my family *in*. If I don't do what he say, he won't kill just *me*, you know? My daughters, my wife. My mother." We were at the river now, and he started backing the boat into the water as he added, "I am very sorry, my new friends."

"Don't feel bad," Ellie said, and put a pale hand on the driver's shoulder. "Feel *good* that you're saving your family." She realized what she had just said in front of me and looked at me with a stricken expression.

"It's okay, Ellie. I'm glad he had a choice. I'd do the same thing." I patted her other hand and just concentrated on how they say you're reunited with the ones you love the most after you die. That would have made our imminent being-eaten-by-a-monster thing a little less horrible. But I doubted it was true.

"*Il existe une différence*," Bonte said, remaining in the driver's seat. "Monsieur Bushnell wants me to take you across in the boat, then leave you and take the boat. I am not going to do that. I am going to go with you, and we will walk out of this jungle together."

"You will not be walking," Cephu said in French, very slowly. "You will all be running." Then he let out a weak laugh and returned to stillness.

Bonte got out of the station wagon and unhooked the boat, settling it into the water before calling to us, "Come, please. Let us give Monsieur Bushnell a show of obeying his orders."

Not seeing any alternative that would keep us alive, Ellie and I opened and got out via our respective doors. Cephu roused himself to open his door and walk stiffly to the motorboat. When he got to Bonte, he said, "He told you to take the boat back, leave us all on the other side? *All* of us?"

Bonte nodded and said, "He did." An idea appeared to our driver. "Cephu—General Cephu—why do we not work together now against Monsieur Bushnell? He wants to kill all these people! He's made *you* and your soldiers kill so many people! Why do we not—"

The gray visage of the general spoke with a firm voice: "Nobody *forced* me to do anything! These miners are vermin, and stupid too. They sell a diamond for five francs so they can buy a skinny chicken for their pots. They embarrass me for my country. I want them all dead and I laugh every time the Kasai Rex eats up a bunch of them and their shit-eating families."

We all stood at the boat, no one moving or even knowing what to say.

"Now *ta gueule* and get in the goddamn boat."

We did, and Bonte manned the outboard motor to get us across the Kasai quickly, shutting it down to allow us to drift right up to the far shore. Ellie and I got out, as did Bonte—but Cephu remained in the boat with a smile on his nauseated visage. "To hell with you and to hell with Bushnell," he said, and pulled on the cord to restart the motor. It rumbled and died. Cephu was just about to pull it again when Bonte spoke up:

"General, they await you on the other side."

Cephu looked up at Bonte quizzically and then glanced over to the part of the shore we had just departed from. Standing there, very still, was an ebony-faced soldier in camo and holding an Uzi that made me wish that Bonte had been able to grab his own. The general seemed to recognize the machine-gun–toting man and shouted to him in the local dialect.

I had no idea what he was yelling, but the soldier definitely heard him. Upon Cephu's completion of his statement (or command, maybe), the soldier turned the Uzi toward us and let fly a hail of bullets that splashed into the water very near the boat and very near the shore.

The general got the message, and jumped out of the boat like a man who hadn't suffered the bloody loss of two pieces of his three-piece set of genitalia. I would have laughed if the bullets hadn't come awfully close to my two friends and me as well. We all lifted our boots toward the hole in the jungle before the soldier with the Uzi decided we needed a fresh dose of motivation.

\*\*\*

If there had been any tracks from the monster or Cephu's henchmen with the stolen eggs, they were washed away in the recent downpour. The clay was still slick and the mud sticky as hell, but we made good progress and by the time I thought to look behind us, the opening in the foliage was no longer visible. Just a couple of minutes ago, Cephu had looked ready to die of sepsis, but now he led our group like a man on a mission. (Which I guess he was, now that he knew how *enthusiastic* Atari was about pushing him into the jungle with us.)

I got the chills when we passed the two trees I had hidden behind that night that seemed so long ago, and I nudged Ellie to look at the giant skull against them. Scavengers and insects had taken every bit of flesh and the jaw had fallen under the rest of the skull once its tendons had been severed and eaten. But it was a skull, and Ellie's eye bugged out as she realized what she was looking at. It was catnip for the host and producer of *Cryptids Alive!*, but cruelly, she had to keep walking and leave it behind. We didn't even have smart phones with cameras on us, nothing to document anything we might see.

Of course, we were very likely to be too dead to share any such documentation with the world anyway. I actually shrugged to myself at these thoughts, and pulled out my penultimate cheroot for a smoke to calm my nerves and let me *think*, goddamn it, but I felt in my back pocket for my matches and remembered I had burned the whole book getting out of my bonds back at Cephu's little party.

Now I was *really* getting depressed. I chucked the unlit cigar into the bushes and trudged at the end of the pack, just looking at my boots as they *splat splat splat* in the mud. I was out of ideas, confused by whether Atari's lies were not lies after all, tired as shit, with burned wrists and a raging hatred of just about everyone and everything at the moment.

It was already dark within the muddy corridor when Cephu veered off the path and through the chaotic growth on the left side. I could just make out a very slight diminishing of the plant life on that side, making a vague path that surely would go unnoticed if one didn't already know it was there. This must have been the route the soldiers took after snatching one of the monster's eggs, one that got them onto the path to the opening and across the river in the quickest way possible. That was probably pretty important when Mama was hot on your heels.

Which was going to be the case with Ellie and me, and now Bonte as well since he joined our merry band of the doomed. I could see Atari's whole scheme now, and it looked as motivated by cruelty and just plain *psychosis* as it was by greed or revenge: he used his connections at The Organization to take vacation time just when I was assigned to the "Kasai Rex" endangered-animal rescue. He got himself ensconced with *Cryptids Alive!* by murdering their cameraman and taking his place. He had already set up the purchase of a majority chunk of Vermeulen stock, maybe with financial partners who had no idea of the machinations to come and thought they were just getting the opportunity to take part in an excellently timed hostile takeover. So, when the main man in his family's company is lost—in reality *shot in cold blood* by Atari but probably thrown into the Kasai River with rocks to keep his body at the bottom and listed as "missing" amidst the massacre of the miners—the stock price plunges and Atari's automated purchase kicks in and *boom*, he's the new owner of the mining arm of Vermeulen International.

That was the logical part of it, at least—but Atari had made it plain that he loved killing the miners and now looked forward to wiping out every one of them currently subcontracted with Vermeulen Mining and replacing them with men operating Caterpillar earth-moving equipment. He hated me for reasons I didn't even understand—and hated The Corporation just as much, for reasons he hadn't even attempted to explain to me beyond being "overworked and underpaid." Did he want me to go on a vendetta against The Corporation because—according to his pose as my Boss—they murdered my wife and son to get my full attention and devotion? Did he want me to despair because they were firing me for becoming a "true believer" and also used their widespread influence to change my identity completely to my cover story?

The only conclusion I was able to reach was that "Atari" Bushnell was out of his goddamned mind, a murderous psychopath very good at doing horrible things for almost no reason and making otherwise clever moves (like the hostile takeover) stained by his complete disregard for human life.

I was no closer to the truth than I was when I set out on this little adventure, but my gaze snapped up from my boots to the direction of a sound I would never have wanted to hear *once*, let alone once again.

It was a drawn-out sibilant, a long and loud *HISSSSSSSSSSSSSSSSSSSSSSSSSSSS*.

Everybody stopped dead. Even Cephu froze in place, and I remembered that he always had his henchmen do his dirty work in the jungle, meaning that *they* probably had ways of avoiding the biggest dangers through sheer repetition, but the general had never personally encountered a Red Megacobra—

Ellie whispered in terrified awe, "That's a Crowing Crested Cobra. They *exist*."

Okay, the general had never personally encountered a Crowing Crested Cobra, but then, neither had any of the rest of us, although of course the prime mover behind *Cryptids Alive!* knew all about it. About its *myth*, anyway, but *this* was as real as the trees around us.

It straightened its body 25 feet high as it hissed, the 10-foot hood around its alien head swelling in anticipation of the meal about to take place. Its enormous forked tongue jabbed out and tasted the delicious air accompanied by an even longer and louder *HISSSSSSSSSSSSSSSSSSSS* that made me want to run for my life, something that would not last for long if I separated myself from the group and presented a moving target for the Megacobra (or whatever the hell it was called) to pounce on, paralyze with its venom, and gobble up.

"*Pourquoi faut-il pas attaquer?*" the general asked Ellie, the woman he and his boys had been ten seconds away from raping and killing just a few hours before: *Why does it not attack?*

Ellie answered in English: "This is my first time at this rodeo myself, Cap'n Crunch."

*She did the thing! With the colloquialisms to annoy the general!* Despite our imminent agonizing deaths, she and I exchanged a smile and surreptitious fist-bump.

"*Quoi?*"

She gave him a break and said in French, "It may not realize we are food ... yet. Or, if it acts like regular-size cobras, it may be petrifying us with fear so that its hatchlings can sneak up and eat us."

*Hatchlings?* How big would the just-hatched offspring of this Mother Of All Snakes have to be—

My question was almost immediately answered by a rustling in the brush to our left, and then also to our right, flanking us while their loving Mum kept us frozen in place. The "babies" made the same move as cobras everywhere, including the three-story-high red one in front of us, standing up their first thirds or so and flapping out their hoods.

I am six-foot-two. The three hatchlings were at least five feet high as they stood in attack mode.

Bonte looked like a ghost. Ellie looked like she didn't know whether to laugh or cry. I felt like I was going to piss myself for the first time since I was in kindergarten. But the general, my God ...

General Cephu looked like he had grabbed a high-voltage wire and was galvanized in place, about to burst into flames from within. He shook as he stared at one of the hatchlings on his side— he was lucky enough to have two while I had "just" one. His eyes were bulging out of his head. I think he might have shit his pants.

The hatchling knew a frightened rabbit when it saw one, and spit a tremendous glob of venom right onto Cephu's crotch. (Maybe it was trying to go for his eyes and wasn't developed enough yet to aim well.) The acid immediately sizzled and ate through the general's camos, not stopping as it turned his penis into bubbling cinders.

I had never heard a scream anything like what General Cephu let out as the venom ate through his dick and then his pelvis. It didn't last long, however—the hatchling moved in and shoved its mouth down and around Cephu's head, yanking him to the ground so he could get all of the fresh meat down its gullet for a nice day of digestion.

We ran. There was one hatchling on the left and one on the right, with Mum right in the middle. I didn't mean to take the lead—I certainly didn't do it consciously—but I did figure that if I went from standing to running as fast as humanly possible, I could get right next to Mum where she couldn't get at me. Running along the mother's flank might also keep the babies from immediately striking, I thought, so I went for it, Bonte and Ellie following like noontime shadows.

It worked. Mum Cobra couldn't see where we had gone at first, and the babies hesitated as we "merged" with her. Their hesitation gave us long enough to get running—as fast as we could through jungle growth, which wasn't terribly fast—and put at least a sporting amount of distance between us and the Megareptiles.

It was too good to last, of course, as Mum got her bearings and twisted around to chase us, the hatchlings following quickly, but not as quickly as their mother. One saving grace was that mother had to get down from her high stance before turning around and giving chase, and any time she wanted to hock another hunk of venom our way, she had to get back up into attack position. This also meant we were another twenty feet away from her, with us on the ground and her that high in the air.

There was another titanic *HISS* and something flew right between Ellie's head and mine, splatting against a huge rock—*a rock*—that instantly started sizzling and melting away and was a quarter of the way dissolved before we even ran past it five seconds later.

*Where were the babies?* We had been so focused on outrunning Mum that the hatchlings were able to flank us in motion and try to hurl themselves onto us. The one on the left launched itself—I did *not* know snakes could do that—and one fang in its open mouth snagged the back of Bonte's safari shirt and ripped it almost all the way off him but missed his dark flesh. He screamed and I'm pretty sure Ellie and I screamed when he screamed. We all continued running and screaming, but everyone was beginning to tire.

"Ellie, what can't snakes do?"

"What?"

"They can swim, they can climb trees—how the hell do you get away from a regular snake? Or a giant one? *Ellie!*"

"I'm thinking!" she yelled, and it looked to me like she was.

"You have to scare it off!" Bonte yelled. "Snakes are afraid of humans!"

"It's true!" Ellie yelled. "Snakes usually attack only when provoked!"

I gave their words a moment to sink in, and, looking behind us while hoping not to trip and die, yelled, "You guys are freaking *insane!* Maybe *normal*-sized snakes are afraid of people, but there's a whole family of *giant* cobras chasing us right ... now ..."

I stopped running. There was no longer anything chasing us. I put my hands on my knees and worked desperately to regain my breath. After a few seconds, Ellie and Bonte joined me in both attempting to get oxygen and also to marvel that we were no longer on the monumental snakes' prey-dar.

"That's it?" I said between breaths. "They quit?"

"What, are you disappointed?" Ellie said, trying to let out a laugh as she hyperventilated. "We must have accidentally walked just past their nest or other safe place. That's why it's so hard for cryptid hunters to—"

"Save it, please," I said, not unkindly, holding up a hand to pause her PSA on the mistreatment of Bigfoot stalkers by the mass media. "General Cephu is Snake Chow now. I'm not sad about that. But he was the only one who knew where we were supposed to go. Shit, we don't even know where we *are*."

"I don't *want* to find the place Cephu was leading us to," Ellie said. "He was taking us to steal eggs from a Kasai Rex so the animal could *eat* us."

I squinted and took a close look around us, turning so that I could take in all 360 degrees to see if I could detect that very subtle path through the jungle that I had noticed before. I saw nothing. And even if I *had* found it, Ellie was right: Why would we want to go to the monster's nest and have the same greeting we just got from the Megacobra?

"My friends, we are between the rock and the hard place," Bonte said, looking at a certain spot I could swear I had looked at closely. "If we go forward, we either get lost and we die. Or if we *don't* get lost, we will find the nest, and Kasai Rex sees us, and we die."

I grumbled, "Well, that's a cheerful—"

"That is not all, Monsieur Brett. If we stop now while there is a little bit of light and manage to miraculously find our way out of the jungle but *without* the egg, Monsieur Bushnell's guard will be waiting, and we die."

Ellie mused, "I don't like the sound of—"

"There is more, Miss White. If we *are* able to steal an egg to avoid being shot, we don't know how to get out of the jungle, the Kasai Rex will find us or we end up fifty kilometers into nowhere, and we die."

I whistled in appreciation of our predicament.

"And finally—"

"Oh, good *Christ*."

Bonte continued, "If we are able to steal an egg to avoid being shot, *and* we are able to outrun the monster, *and* we are able to get out of the jungle, *then* we will be responsible for the Kasai Rex killing the miners, all of whom will be locked out of the safe building."

We stood in silence for a moment, or for what passed as silence in the African rainforest. "So," Ellie said, "should we just kill ourselves right now?"

I would have expected Bonte to smile at that, but he was not in "jolly taxi driver" mode. He shook his head somberly and said, "Monsieur Bushnell does not expect us to make it back alive. He surely has soldiers and a new general who will be carrying back an egg if we do not show up. They know how to get through the jungle very fast back to the camp with *le monstre* right behind them. Thus, if we kill ourselves now, Miss Ellie, all of the miners will die and 'Atari' will get everything he wants."

"You're depressing the shit out of me," I said.

"I am sorry, Monsieur Brett."

I put my hands on my hips, and I could feel the slight tightness in my belt due to the .45 jammed in back. But even if my bullets could hurt, let alone kill, the rampaging Kasai Rex, we'd have to find it first—and we'd have to find it while there was still even the meager amount of light we got on the ground from the canopy above.

I looked all around us for any signs of Mega-*anything*, cobras or crocodiles or spiders or name-your-cryptid—*God, why couldn't this have just been a regular extraction like my last hundred assignments?*—and, seeing nothing, I just looked at the ground. Actually, there was a noticeably greater illumination of the patch of jungle we were standing in at that moment. It wasn't *bright* by any means, but you could have read the top of an eye chart by it, and that was quite a difference right there.

That made me look up at the treetops, and of course that prompted Ellie and Bonte to look as well. Apparently not seeing anything in particular, they both lowered their gazes to me, and finally I returned them. "The trees are a little thinner here, am I right in that?"

Bonte looked up and Ellie looked down, and both of them looked at me again and nodded.

Good, it wasn't just me. Because I also noted that our little relative amount of clearing was wide enough for even a very large dinosaur-like animal to stomp through. And though it was hard to discern, I believed that I could make out the clearing extending a little ways before making a bend.

"I think we're on a path. *The* path."

Bonte said, "I don't see a path, my friend. I see a random jungle arrangement."

I said to Ellie, "Do you see anything?"

She screwed up her lips and shrugged.

"Do you have a plan?" I asked Bonte, knowing obviously his speech of thirty seconds earlier showed he didn't have any such thing.

"I do not."

"We do now—I think this is a path, and I think we should follow it. We got nothing else, and I don't feel like just standing around and waiting for our inevitable deaths."

Ellie smiled and motioned for me to take the lead. "After you, Mister Optimism."

Bonte laughed at that, and I did too, no matter how shit-scared I was that this "path" might turn out to be nothing … or it might turn out to be the exact thing to lead us to the nest of the Kasai Rex. What would happen then, as they said around these parts, was up to the ancestors.

# CHAPTER 16

It *was* a path. Not clearly defined like the hole at the edge of the Kasai River near the mines, but there was no mistaking that whatever trees and other obstacles that might be leveled by a running lizard monster were gone. Mossy stumps big enough to trip a human (or stop him entirely) were all over the place, but the trees that once stood open them had either been knocked into the thicker jungle on either side or left where they fell to rot and be trampled again and again into mush.

But what was this a path *to*? Confirmation bias—oh yes, I had become intimately familiar with every logical fallacy one could use to get what he wants—told me that because the path was wide enough for a monster of the size I judged to have bitten through that Megapython, well, then it had to be a path the monster had forged.

This was a dangerous and stupid fallacy to be tricked into when hunting "cryptids," which never were what the locals thought it was. So I was not going to fall for it now. This could be an old path, something abandoned, even if it were at one time used by my Kasai Rex. But it's all we had, so we continued to follow it. Actually, it was becoming even more clearly a thoroughfare of some kind, *probably* for animals but could have been salted during World War II to allow troops to move through. It was something to follow, though, like I said, so we followed, even if we were just to have something to do.

"I thought this was gonna be a crocodile. Not even an endangered one," I said to Ellie, who smiled ruefully.

"I thought maybe we'd find some spoor, some little clues." She sighed. "Everybody knows we never actually find anyth—"

"*Baba zangu*," Bonte said in astonishment.

"Yeah," I mumbled in the same tone, "what he said."

We were looking at another river. What we had been walking on, what the path had transversed, was an island. This was the Kasai again, flowing slower and so wide here we could just barely see the other shore.

"Does anyone have an iPhone?" I said, not tearing my eyes away from the vista in front of us.

"I have Google Android," Bonte said.

"Oh, good, can I borrow—"

"But I do not use it."

"What? Why not?"

"No service out here."

"Oh, of course, duh," I said, figuring he would understand the sentiment.

"Also, it is back in the Vermeulen wagon."

"Okay."

"Plus, it is also broken and has no battery."

Before I could scream, Ellie said, "God, I wish we had the satellite phone," Ellie said. "I know Atari compromised it, but we could use it as a hotspot for our phones. Are you dying to call in your discovery, Sir Richard?"

I gave her a smile at that but said, "No, I want to see a satellite view of this place. I never thought to survey the region, just looked at the map of Tshikapa and the mines, noting that it was right next to a deep tributary of the Congo, and so it was a croc dragging people off." Goddamn confirmation bias. No need to look at the rest of the map! *Moron.*

"I have a map," Bonte said.

I didn't even say anything this time, just looked at him, waiting.

"However, it is in the car."

"Of course it is."

"And I think this part of the river is not on it. I use it for driving in Tshikapa."

Ellie intervened. "The path you noticed, Brett ... it basically stretches right through this island, connecting one side with the other."

"Huh, yes, right." It was one of those statements that sounds like utter trivia until you think about it ... and then you realize it answers a lot of questions.

"Kasai Rex is said to be essentially amphibian," the cryptid hunter said. "And the giant crocodile and python you saw ... no one has ever seen the crocodiles, even though they're enormous, because they're semi-aquatic and nest on *this* side of the island."

"What about the Megapython? Why didn't we see any of its eggs?"

"Their birthing season is done. Same with the cobras."

"Yeah, I do seem to recall some 'baby' cobras," I said, maybe with a bit of sarcasm.

"So what you are saying," Bonte interjected cautiously, "is that we are standing exactly where these giant killer animals come up onto the island."

Ellie and I jumped and ran out of the path like we had just realized we were standing on a trap door. Bonte followed us with a chuckle, but none too slowly himself.

"This explains why the soldiers can get at the Kasai Rex's eggs so easily," Ellie said, and ventured to place one foot just beyond the waterline and peer into some reeds and mud a few feet down the shore, where none of us could quite reach. "My god, there they are. They're *huge*."

She stepped aside to allow me a look and yes indeed, the soldier I saw was carrying something right about that size, and it seemed heavy as hell, too. "How do we know these aren't giant crocodile eggs?" Ellie asked, giving me a chance to be the smart one.

"Crocs hide their eggs in the mud, pretty much covering them. I imagine Megacrocodiles would protect their eggs in the same manner," I said, and waited for Ellie to be impressed.

It would have been a long wait.

Bonte also wanted to take a look at the eggs, and even he whistled at their size. "*Cela ressemble à de la merde lourde*," he said, then translated to me: "That looks like some heavy shit."

We had a laugh over that, but one question seemed to occur to us all at the same moment. Ellie put it into words: "So where's Mama?"

We didn't have much time to ponder this—although my answer would have been "lurking in the river, deciding whether to swallow us individually or as a group"—because there was a stirring in the jungle behind us of a kind that didn't seem like snakes or panthers or anything else that represented the "normal" imminent death available in the Congo rainforest.

No, now we could hear low voices. These were humans. I glanced at the setting sun, and I knew *which* humans. It was the militia soldiers, come to make their final theft of the Kasai Rex's egg and bring an end to the miners, however many dozens or hundreds had remained resolutely behind at the mine. They didn't have us in their line of sight yet, so I silently indicated to Bonte and Ellie that we needed to get into the foliage for cover, and *fast*.

Fortunately for us, right off the path and far away from the eggs, we would be difficult to spot if they didn't know someone was already there, and maybe if they did know. The soldiers—four of them this time, probably to grab more eggs to put an exclamation point on the theft for Mama—stopped and leaned against some mossy trees on the other side of the path, chatting and lighting cigarettes to smoke as they waited for the sun to go all the way down. The darkness made the Kasai Rex attacks that much more horrifying, and they were going for maximum horror here. I could see the miners, six people thick, screaming and pounding uselessly on the formerly welcoming door of Vermeulen Mining.

I wondered if Atari would use the security cameras to laugh at them. He was winning all the marbles, wasn't he? And he had messed with my mind so much I didn't know if I was fired or if my employer had killed my family or … anything at all, really. I didn't even know for sure if I would even be able to get back home, even if I miraculously didn't get weren't snatched up in this cryptid's crushing jaws.

Or was I actually texting with the Boss, and this was Atari's overarching mind game? Did they kill my family? Did they poach animals themselves for millionaires? I could scarcely believe either of those … but the doubt was planted in my mind by that fat son of a bitch, and now I was in no place to find out what was what. I guess if the Boss refused to take my call, that would be an answer in itself …

I shook those thoughts away. First things first, and the first thing here was *not dying*.

So we hid. We had to see how the soldiers got the monster's attention after they stole the eggs, to get her to come after them, raging and roaring.

It got darker, darker, and finally it was night. The men had flashlights—it was thanks to those that I saw anything at all when trapped in the jungle—and they flicked them on as they approached the nest. They must have felt pretty confident in their egg-snatching prowess, since they didn't stop chattering the whole time. I was right—they had more men because they were taking more eggs for the big finale, trying to piss off the Kasai Rex to the absolute max.

I turned to Bonte and asked him *very* quietly what the men were saying.

"*Ce sont des animaux*," he whispered back, sounding hollow. "Nothing more than animals."

That sounded less than optimal. I imagine they were discussing the upcoming slaughter with light hearts and chuckles, and I hated them.

Now that it was dark, cigarette butts were discarded and the men formed a bucket brigade not ten feet in front of us, the two soldiers closest to the next up to their knees in the water and balancing very carefully to stay standing on the muddy bank and not fatally slide into the river, and the last one holding a flashlight to guide the rest. The first man bent at the knees, soaking the seat of his pants but getting maximum leverage to lift the first egg out of the nest, which I could see contained five more, tall ovoids each as tall as a dining room's master chair and probably twice as heavy.

It seemed to me insanely reckless to be shining a flashlight around the nest, sure to bring Mama's attention earlier than I would think they'd want. This was especially true because we could see quite well by the light of the moon here at the edge of the water. But before any stir came from the river, they had handed off three of the eggs, just as I thought they would with four men. What the soldier who picked the eggs from the nest did next made my mouth drop open with surprise … and then I realized it was genius.

The soldier grabbed one final egg—and chucked it as far as he could manage, swinging it granny-style from between his legs, into the river, where it sank like a stone.

Then all four of them, the first three hauling one enormous egg each, took off like their feet were on fire.

I saw a heaving in the water, and a hint of a tremendous tail in the moonlight. A *tail?* I wondered why the monster would be diving instead of crawling out of the water to chase the thieves, but *of course*: she heard and saw the egg go into the river and sink. She would dive to rescue that egg and place it back into the nest ... and then she would see that three of the eggs were missing.

A sniff of the air would tell her what direction the thieves ran in, and the Kasai Rex would be after them—and would destroy every living thing in the tent city until she found all of her well-hidden eggs.

I figured we had about twenty seconds until Mama rose to put the egg back into the nest. We had to act *now* or we wouldn't have a chance to act at all.

"What the hell do we *do*?" Ellie pleaded at a whisper, pulling on my shirtsleeve to emphasize her words. "If the cryptid follows the soldiers, everyone dies and Atari wins!"

"I know, I know ..." We needed more time. But how could I buy us more time?

I jumped up from our hiding place in reflex, before my sudden plan had been able to travel from my brain to my feet. I waded into the water, bent awkwardly to reach one of the remaining eggs—Bonte was right behind me, so he was able to help before I snapped my back—and he and I lifted it out of the nest. And ... *oh my God.*

The monster surfaced from the river, a giant fanlike structure poking through first and then the rest of her coming up behind it. In seconds, we could see the full length of the beast we were facing. And the sail, that huge sail on her, immediately identified our "cryptid" to me. This wasn't a Kasai Rex, wasn't a cryptid at all, in fact—

*It was a dinosaur.* A spinosaurus.

My son's favorite, in fact, because it was the hugest and the most fierce, the alpha predator that could break a T. rex's neck if it felt like it. My boy's favorite movie was *Jurassic Park III*, and this big bitch was the star of that movie, which I had been forced to watch on video ten thousand times (and wished now I could watch with him even one more time, but no time for any of that now). In the movie, spinosaurus was a biped, but the creature before us was obviously a four-legged killer, looking like The Mother of all Crocodiles. She floated casually toward her nest, a place we needed to get out of before she saw that other eggs were missing.

"Spinosaurus," I said in awe to Bonte and especially Ellie, who was crouched right at the shoreline listening to us. "The neural spines are the giveaway."

"A dinosaur?" Ellie smiled widely. "A lesson from Harry Junior."

I smiled, too, because it was. Then I shared another lesson: "Remember when General Cephu told us the monster—our spinosaur—could smell ... um, fellow Africans?"

They nodded.

"The spinosaur, like T. rex, relies mostly on smell and on motion in its visual field. If we can overpower the soldiers' particular scent, we can make her chase *us* instead."

Bonte's eyes popped out in alarm, but Ellie only nodded, getting me immediately. "If we can get her—*her*, funny, I didn't think of the cryptid like that—to follow, at most three people die because she will have lost the scent to chase the soldiers back to the mine."

"Exactly."

Bonte waited just a beat before he spurted, "So what now?" in a tone of voice moving quickly toward panic, and I took the heavy egg from him.

"You run—*run*—back to the camp and get the miners out of there, just have them run through the city, to the airport, anywhere far enough from wherever those assholes are hiding those eggs. Go now!" As he ran off down the clearing after the soldiers, I picked up a dead sharp piece of branch from the jungle floor, pressed it against the shell, murmured, "God, please forgive me," and punctured a fist-sized chunk out of it. "ELLIE, *RUN!*"

The spinosaur was just placing her rescued egg from her mouth into the nest. We ended up timing it just right—we ran as fast as the mud would allow just as Mama was distracted by her discovery that there were *more* eggs missing. She sniffed the air for information, then screamed her roar of unbridled *fury*, because what she could smell was the life fluid draining from the hole-punched egg I held as Ellie and I ran like demons.

We didn't follow the clearer path, since that led back to the camp. Instead, we veered off into the tree-heavy area of the island. The spinosaurus was going to have to get past a lot of heavy woods to get at us. I hoped the trees would at least slow her down a little bit, because I snatched a quick glance or two at the impossible dinosaur now pulling herself out of the water to come after us. She was fifty feet long at least, and taller than the Vermeulen Mining building even before taking her giant sail into account. She stood on four thick legs and her snout was long, made for catching sea creatures but also well-suited for eating up more land-based, mammalian types like screaming humans. Which I believe we were about to be.

Ellie must have snuck a look as well, because she breathed out, "It's magnificent."

I thought I had heard the dinosaur *ROAR* and *GROWL* earlier, but that was nothing like the blast she gave now, shaking the trees themselves, as she smelled her baby's essence flowing out of the egg, the life dripping away. I felt terrible about killing one of her eggs, but if it was the only hope I had that she'd follow us to wherever instead of following the soldiers to the tent city, then it was a load of bad karma I was willing to bear.

We ran then, staying near the shoreline so we wouldn't get lost, but enough away from the water that the dinosaur would have to get through the trees. Ellie had to get her small but powerful flashlight out of her khakis so we could see what was directly in front of us, at least. There were roots and tangles of vines and huge nocturnal bugs which made my skin crawl, but nothing we couldn't get past as yet. We needed the flashlight to see in front of us, but the spinosaur was huge enough to have her outline illuminated to visibility by the moon.

She definitely was coming after us and not following the soldiers on the usual trail, and when she hit the first clutch of trees, it sounded like a bomb going off. I chanced a look back again and saw that she had broken the trees she ran into, but they weren't sheared down to the stump to allow her passage yet. She backed up a bit and hurled herself at the treeline again, this time busting through with her massive bulk and muscles and *rage*.

This was good news for us, because every foot we could put between her and ourselves was step closer to … I was going to say "survival," but I didn't even know if that was an option on the table. We just continued to *run* as the dinosaur crashed through the trees … and then stopped. It took us a few seconds to notice, then a few more seconds to stop and look behind us.

There was no sign of the spinosaurus in the woods now. Trying to catch her breath, Ellie gasped, "Where'd it go—"

Her question was overwhelmed by the blast of *HRRRRRRRRANNNNNNNNNNNHHHHHH* coming from the spinosaur, who had changed her direction of pursuit and was now almost perpendicular to us. She had given up on trying to mow down the trees between her and us, instead using her amphibian nature to propel herself up the muddy shore, catching up to where we were, but separated ninety feet or so from us because of the trees and jungle foliage near the water line. If there was any kind of clearing ahead that the spinosaur could slip through to us, we were dead.

At this point, we weren't really running so much as semi-rapidly weaving our way through the jungle, faster than the spinosaur could have busted through the trees after us, but now she was throwing her bulk into the thick growth between us, knocking down some big trunks but then running parallel to us as we desperately scrambled over obstacles big and small.

She kept pace but couldn't get to us as of yet. However, she would find a way where there was less between her and us, and it was obvious she was smart—and enraged—enough to bide her time.

Ten more minutes went by with us climbing over and under the riotous foliage when Ellie said with weakened breath, "Brett, where are we *going*? We can't keep this up much longer."

She was saying exactly what I was thinking. It was an island in the Kasai, that much we had determined along with its width at the point of the path, but its length was something we had no idea about. Were we nearing the north of the island, where we could cut and head back toward the mines? My idea was that we would lead Mama to the mines on the side *opposite* the river, so that she could find the eggs the soldiers had placed there to ensure maximum destruction and leave off the chase in time for us to somehow get into that bunker building and wait out the fury of the dinosaur.

I didn't have anywhere near the breath to tell her all of this, but she trusted me and I would repay that trust by not doing anything insane. We'd continue north for a few more miles and then ...

*Oh, bloody hell.* There were lights ahead, bright lights, the kind of lights that are meant to illuminate a wide area like a sports field. And since I doubted anyone had set up a baseball diamond here on a distant point on the island, it could only be one thing up ahead:

Soldiers. The militia that planned to seize the mines along with our old friend Atari.

I could guess from my commando days that they had cleared a part of the forest where they could set up a small base from which to make secret raids and cause mayhem among the miners and maybe even the rest of the population of Tshikapa. They weren't visible here, and five would get you ten that their clearing included a nice smooth area for boats to be pushed from and also to be dragged onto so they weren't seen or damaged.

That meant this part of the rainforest was about to thin out and then disappear entirely for a stretch, exactly what our prehistoric predator needed to get at the thieves who had the smell of her baby's fluids all over them. We couldn't just turn left and run into the jungle, because we would become hopelessly lost without any chance the sheer luck of finding the path the dinosaur had cleared out over God knew how many trips back and forth. We had to keep moving forward, north with the spinosaurus now just fifty feet or so away, scrambling up the waterline to keep pace with us.

What do you do when you can't go forward and you can't go back? You *stop.*

I shut off the flashlight—there was plenty of illumination from the militia base two hundred feet ahead of us—and held out an arm across Ellie to slow her down, the egg being empty enough for me to carry with the other arm. We stopped running and she didn't need me to put a finger to my lips to remind her to stay quiet. We stopped and took in lungfuls of air, even though the stitches running through us didn't allow for much at first.

Mama must have thought we were still running, because she continued her thumping and sliding up the shore until she got to the base. The unholy *ROAR* sounded again, and immediately I heard men shouting amidst gunfire, AK-47s emptying their magazines into the tremendous spinosaurus. I couldn't see if the weapons had any effect on the beast, but I could hear that they hadn't stopped her entirely. She let loose another ground-shaking shriek of utter violence and fury, and then I heard men not shouting anymore but *screaming*.

Our girl must not have been hungry, because as we crept closer we could see that she wasn't bothering to swallow the soldiers, instead just impaling them on her teeth, crushing them into pulp with a couple of bites, and then tossing their pieces and parts wherever as she went at another victim.

"Can we get away now?" Ellie asked. "I think I don't like actually *finding* a cryptid."

I breathed a laugh at that, and the same question had occurred to me. Should we ditch the almost-empty shell of the egg and try to get back to the mines? Was there any danger that the dinosaur would continue to follow us, meaning that going back to the camp would put the miners in the danger we had just tried to save them from? And if we *didn't* go back, would Atari and his men just do this again tomorrow night? We couldn't play cat-and-mouse with the spinosaur forever, and bullets didn't even seem to bother her, let alone kill her.

Fortunately, there were a lot of militia soldiers for Mama to take her rage out on. We snuck a little closer even as she turned the clearing red with blood, guts, and body parts. That's when one miner chose our exact location to run through to get away from the slaughter.

I saw my opportunity. It was a terrible opportunity to take, but I took it.

I work to protect animals and, whenever possible, people. But I was willing to do horrible things for good ends. As the soldier came crashing through our part of the brush, I stepped in front of him, and knocked him down with the egg, splashing the remainder of the amniotic fluid all over him. He sputtered in panic, but I calmed him down by saying in my rudimentary French (I could understand more than I could produce), "Take this flashlight and go this way"—I indicated the south, the direction from which we had come—"along the water and you will be safe."

He understood my words, already crying with gratitude and relief, and took the flashlight and cut across the fifty feet or so of undergrowth and trees to the muddy bank and took a hard right turn. I felt like the most horrible person in the world … until I remembered that he and his compatriots were going to use the monster to kill more than a hundred people so they could make money. Then I didn't feel so bad.

I could hardly believe it myself, but my slapdash idea worked: the spinosaurus stopped shaking her head and flinging what remained of human bodies and sniffed the air. *She could smell her egg again.* She unleashed another *ROAR*, but this one was shortened by her almost immediate run after the scent of her baby—a chase which would be aided greatly by the soldier's recent acquisition of a nicely moving and trackable flashlight.

"What now?"

God, I was really hating that question, mostly because I was asking it of myself even as I heard the words come from Ellie. It wouldn't take the dinosaur long to crunch the life out of that poor militia soldier, and then she would be without a trail to follow, except maybe if she could pick up our original scent. Either way, we needed to get through this cluster of gun-toting soldiers if we were to …

I stopped and listened. No one was screaming. No one was even talking. I chanced a slow approach to the very edge of the base's clearing and all I could see was death. Not one soldier stirred. The ones who had been to avoid being ravaged may have been hiding inside their Quonset hut, or perhaps had fled into the jungle themselves. And they had left something behind:

A Jeep.

\*\*\*

It was spattered with blood and maybe some guts—it was hard to make out exactly what was what, and that was actually a bit of a blessing—but the Jeep had keys in it and started right up, shining its excellent high-beam headlights. Ellie looked a bit worried about "What now?" even though she didn't actually ask the question again. She was no wilting flower, but I had seen war and she hadn't; I had killed men and suicide-bomb–armed women and she hadn't; I had needed to escape or die, and until now, she hadn't. So this strong woman did what strong people everywhere did—she let someone with more experience take charge, at least for the moment. It had nothing to do with the size of her breasts and everything to do with the size of her intellect. I really liked this girl.

If she had asked the question "What now?" old loud, however, I would have answered it very quickly by reminding her that no one needed a Jeep to get around a baseball-diamond–sized militia base. No, there had to be a path wide enough for a Jeep. The militia might have gotten this single Jeep to the island on some kind of ad hoc barge or wide raft, but they would need it here only if they were going to need some fast transportation from one part to another. (I was thinking from their base to where they could harass Vermeulen's company and miners and back.) There was no path in the jungle from whence Ellie and I had just come, and the Jeep certainly wouldn't have been able to drive along the mostly submerged mud of the waterline to the south, so their driving path had to be somewhere over—

*There!* I saw the clearing between the jungle and the river's edge, just wide enough for a vehicle. The militia must have cleared (or had cleared by paying the men who cleared it a dollar a day, less than the slave wages the militia protested at the mines) a path from this part of the island to somewhere on the side facing the mine.

In the distance, a horrible roar, a terror-filled scream, and then nothing for a few seconds. Then came a shrieking animal wail of anger and despair.

"She's coming back," Ellie said.

"Let's not be here," I said and took off toward the shoreline path. If I were wrong and this was *not* a path cleared all the way around the north side for this Jeep, we would crash and maybe drown, maybe be ripped apart by Mama. But we'd definitely be dead.

I stepped on the gas and we flew down the muddy clearance. The headlights showed only clear path ahead and I applied as much speed as I could without flinging us into the river at any sudden turn. We were making good time. Even if the spinosaur made her way back to the soldiers' original egg-theft clearing through the island—and she would, since that's where her remaining eggs sat in their muddy nest—maybe she wouldn't be able to get to the river and the mine on that side before we could find the three eggs and put them right where she could find them before entering the camp and killing every goddamned living thing there.

We were moving right along when an *ERNKK* sounded from our back axle and our speed noticeably lowered. Ellie and I gave each other a "What the hell?" look and she kneeled backward on her seat to see what was going on back there at the same time I tried to see what I could in my mirrors.

"No! No, no, *no!*" Ellie shouted half-pleadingly, half in anger.

"What is—" I started to ask, but then caught a glimpse of red rope dragging behind the Jeep. Or not rope. It looked more like …
*no.*

The powerful baby Megacobra used its upper body and jaw muscles to hurl the end of its body forward into the backseat of the open Jeep, then released the axle and swept its cowled head and neck inside as well.

As Ellie screamed and looked around frantically for something to kill the giant snake—or hurt it, or at the very least make it fall out of the Jeep—it reared back and I knew it was ready to spit its venom. I yanked Ellie down to put her seat between her and the snake, and I ducked down as far as I could and still stay on the road.

Seconds later a *thump* struck the back of my seat and the smell of melting vinyl overwhelmed us. Luckily for me, the spit wasn't as strong as Mum's, because I would have now had a hole eaten through my chest, where I keep many important organs. Ellie screamed again, and that was fine. My blood was throbbing so hard in my ears from sheer adrenaline that I could barely hear her or anything else, but hunkered down I saw something even more amazing than giant snakes and dinosaurs:

There was a .45 held on by magnets under the base of the steering column. It must have been put there in case the militia was stopped and their guns confiscated, allowing the driver to surprise their attackers by putting bullets in their heads.

I grabbed the .45, switched off the safety, and handed it to Ellie. At first she looked shocked and then she nodded, whipped herself back into visibility, and squeezed off five shots in rapid succession. The snake made a choking hiss and fell right off the back of the Jeep.

"Nice shootin', Annie Oakley!"

"I took some self-defense clas—*AIEEEEEEEE!*" her sentence being cut off by her piercing scream, which was followed by a *dunk* into the backseat. It was the other baby red Megacobra.

"Oh, come the hell *ON!*"

Ellie popped back up and unloaded the rest of the bullets into this one, and it slumped dead inside the Jeep. This was good and bad *and* good: it was good that our latest snake friend was dead; but bad because its weight was immense and slowed the Jeep considerably; but good because the extra weight gave us better traction on the always-slippery track running alongside the river.

Oh, and *bad* because here was their enraged two-story–high mother, blocking the road. "This is *not* how cobras hunt," I said, out of ideas and just about out of patience: my adrenaline had been at full capacity for an hour now and this sudden stop brought it down immediately and precipitously. My hands shook and it was hard to keep my eyes open. I didn't know what to do or even how to say "I'm sorry" to Ellie.

The full-grown Megacobra stood even a little taller as it collected its venom, the first glob of which would eat through the hood and the engine, or through the windshield and our bodies. It reared all the way back and—

*RAT-TAT-TAT-TAT-TAT-TAT!   RRRRAT-TAT-TAT-TAT-TAT-TAT-TAT!*

Ellie had jumped forward and engaged the loaded 105mm M40 recoilless rifle bolted onto our windshield assembly. The casings flying everywhere and landing hot on my head and the seat and the dead cobra in the backseat, Ellie used up the entire belt of ammunition feeding into the machine gun. When she was done, I was no longer shaking—my adrenaline was back!—but she looked almost overcome with shock. She plopped back into her seat in time for us to watch the cryptid's top half fall off its bottom half into the water, severed entirely by Ellie's barrage of high-powered bullets.

It was a sight no one ever thought they'd see, I'm sure, but I had to bring the party down by pointing out, "Nice work, but now we've got at least two tons of dead snake blocking the road."

Ellie put her face in her hands, not crying but probably on the verge.

I heard something stirring in the water, and I shut the headlights off. Yes—there was a splash, then a growl-snarl, then another, then more splashing, and then that tell-tale exhalation of a lion's roar: crocodiles.

As my eyes adjusted more to the dark and we could see by the moonlight, I spotted them, two regular size (although massive) Nile crocs were rolling and ripping the flesh from the part of the cobra that had dropped into the water.

"Of course," I whispered. "All that blood in the water is going to attract every crocodile within—"

Something huge—at least compared to the crocs in the water—came out of the jungle to our left and opened its jaws as far as they could go, then clamped down on the rest of the dead cobra's carcass and dragged it back into the dark with it. Ellie and I could see it only by the moonlight, but I knew what it was because I had seen it before.

It was the Megacrocodile, and whether it was taking revenge for its swallowed-whole mate or just hungry for a giant pile of fresh meat, it cleared the path for us, slicker than ever with the snake's hundred gallons of blood spilled on it. But that was all right—we had our dead baby Megacobra in the backseat to keep up from sliding off the road.

"Megacrocodiles," Ellie murmured in awe. "They're real."

"And very helpful to the island traveler," I said with a smile as I popped the headlights back on. "I must remember to write a thank-you letter to the Congo Motor Club."

Ellie laughed, and that was a good sound to hear. The only thing now was to get to the mine site before our spinosaur did ... if it wasn't already too late.

# CHAPTER 17

Shortly after our encounter with the Cobra Family, the path took a turn to the south, meaning we had crossed the north side of the Kasai River island and were heading toward the Vermeulen Mining camp. This was the first real measure we had of the size of the island: it was small but large enough to contain more diversity than I would have thought possible. Of course, the diversity was made up of stupendous-sized predators who I would bet anything spent most of their time on the other side of the river from the mine and from where the dinosaur had (very unfortunately) set up her nest of eggs. That was all completely unexplored by man. Maybe as humans ate up more rainforest, there would be some new surprises from those already inhabiting it.

Or whatever. I had no time to keep pondering because some fifteen minutes of careful driving later, we reached the end of the clearing, where the riotous plant life once again spread right to the waterline. This was expected, since for some time we could see the lights across the river of Tshikapa, so we knew we were nearing the mine.

I brought the Jeep to a stop, and there it was, the motorboat the militia used to go back and forth from the mainland. Without explanation, I rushed Ellie into the boat, hopped in myself, and pushed against the shore to move us silently away from the Jeep.

"What's the hurry, sailor?" Ellie said, smiling despite herself.

"This boat being here wasn't completely a good sign," I said quietly.

She lowered her voice to match mine. "What? Why, did you want to swim the rest of the way?"

I looked behind us as we chugged from the shore. "If the boat was already here, that means those four militia guys have already planted the eggs ... and they expected to see the Jeep there to take them back to their island base."

"Then why didn't they kill us when they saw it wasn't their pals?" Ellie said.

"I think maybe they were dragging ass like tired soldiers everywhere. Look."

She turned to see for herself, and we were still close enough that we could see that the four militia members must have been just within the jungle, maybe taking a quick rest while they waited for their ride, when we pulled up and I ushered us into the boat, because as if on cue, they stepped out of the darkness and got in the vehicle.

Well, two of them did—the other two jumped back at the half a giant snake carcass in the back. The two in front laughed like hell and made a motion that said *Suck it up and get in*, and the two perched uncomfortably on the dead snake as best they could.

They were all in the Jeep and attempting to turn it around to go back in the direction of their camp, so I took a chance and pulled on the outboard's chain to bring the motor to live. I don't think the egg-thieving soldiers in the Jeep even heard it, and even if they did, we were around the bend and out of their sight within seconds.

It wasn't even a mile by my estimation before we had Tshikapa and the mines on our right and the crazy monster island on the left. We were so beyond shell-shocked that I, at least, couldn't form any kind of statement about it, or even a question. Ellie seemed exactly the same. All we could focus on was, once we were near the mine shore and I cut the engine, sliding up as quietly as possible.

It was, as usual, utterly dark except for the security lights on the Vermeulen building. We would have to tread very carefully around the dozens of deep holes the poor miners had dug with their bare hands in search of the rough stones. All seemed extremely quiet, which both reassured me and made me nervous at the same time—that meant the soldiers must have *just* placed the eggs, giving us at least a little time to find them and put them on the shore, maybe even in the boat for easy access for Mama. But it wasn't good in a way, because Mama would probably not look kindly on Ellie and me—and Bonte, if we could all find one another in the darkness—carrying her eggs, even if it was to put them back where she could get them. (I don't claim to be an expert on dinosaur psychology, but I'm thinking the greatest predator of the Cretaceous Period isn't going to let an apparent lack of motive stand in the way or swift and terrible retribution.)

We made it past the mines themselves and now were walking between the tents. Snoring sounded all around and feet poked out from some of them. Why hadn't Bonte gotten them out, like he was supposed to? Anywhere would have to be safer for the miners than here.

As if on cue, a tree-shaking *HRRRRRRRANNNNNNNNNNNHHHHHH!!!*

From the jungle across the river.

Mama was coming.

The sound brought the entire tent city awake at once. There was little screaming, just barked instructions between families and the scooping up anything especially precious, like a child or a metal shovel.

"Where the hell is Bonte?" I said in angry exasperation to Ellie, who was also looking around for any sign of our driver and friend. His assistance was essential because Atari said that he would be bolting the doors of the bunker—

The first miners to reach the door were now discovering that it was not opening and no one was answering the intercom at the door. Then the security lights went out altogether and the screaming finally did start.

"Bre-h-h-h-h-t," came a singsong voice very near me. "E-l-l-i-e-e-e-e ..."

A walkie-talkie was on the ground not fifteen feet away from us, but of course we couldn't see it without turning on the flashlight, and another piercing roar from the jungle, closer now, made doing that a bad idea. It was, of course, Atari: "I can see you two."

We spun around, looking for him in the dark.

"From inside, dumbasses. With my infrared."

"I thought General Cephu smashed your infrared."

"I'm not even going to dignify that idiocy with a response," Atari said, actually sounding a little miffed now. "You have about, I'd wager, one minute before the Kasai Rex—"

Ellie said, "Actually, it's a Spinosaurus—"

"Actually, shut your mouth, bitch. You got about a minute until *the monster* comes and kills every single person closer than the guard station. If you want to live, I'll let you in the building through the concealed door."

All of the miners and their families were screaming now, begging in whatever language or dialect came to them in their panic. They beat at the door and even at the concrete around the door, clawed at it. No one was getting in, and they were truly realizing that now.

Except Ellie and I could still get in. We could still survive. *She* could still survive.

"You go," I told her. "You get inside and I'll grab the eggs and try to appease Mama as much as possible."

"Smart man," Atari mocked through the walkie-talkie, "except it's both or nobody. Forty-five seconds now."

I could hear the crashing stomps of the enraged spinosaurus. It really wouldn't be long.

"Oh, hey, while you're thinking about my offer, shine your flashlight over here," his voice said from the walkie-talkie.

I did. The spotlight showed that our friend Bonte had it strapped to his head even as he lay bound at the hands and feet with duct tape, more tape keeping his mouth sealed.

"Ain't no way my brother there is gonna make it unless you guys bring him inside. No time to cut his tape and run with him. Shit, he can't even roll his way to safety. No trees to hide behind here. Now get your asses around the building and cut this shit. I have uses for you. The Organization doesn't anymore … as far as you know."

I didn't even bother to shout extremely impolite words at Atari through the walkie-talkie. I just got my hands under Bonte—and thank God he was a skinny Congolese instead of our fat American—and hurled him onto my shoulders, to carry him fireman-style.

"I know where the eggs are!" Ellie shouted, like a light bulb had literally just popped on in her head. "The guardhouse! Atari said people would die 'up to the guardhouse'!"

"Let's move!" I said, and we did, Ellie taking the flashlight and keeping it on. It wouldn't make much difference in a few seconds when the dinosaur emerged from the jungle and slid into the water to get at us.

"It's not gonna do you any good!" Atari shouted from the walkie-talkie, and so Ellie's deduction was confirmed and we ran faster.

"Ellie, get the miners toward the gate, past the guard station. *HURRY!*" I yelled at her, and she peeled off with the flashlight and started screaming at them in her very high-pitched shout, "*Courir à travers la porte d'entrée!*" That, along with her motioning with the flashlight, seemed to get through to every screaming person at once, and they moved as a panicked mass toward the front gate. It was just in time, too, *maybe* just in time, because the spinosaurus now cleared that hole in the jungle and let out a horrendous screech. She made a huge splash as she jumped into the water—no elegant sliding now—and would be on our side in seconds.

At the front of the camp, the lights from Tshikapa gave enough illumination for me to see by. Setting Bonte down and pulling the tape from his mouth, I made it to the guardhouse and remembered as I saw them that there were *three* eggs. I couldn't carry three eggs—I wasn't totally sure I could carry two of the big bastards. I wrapped my hand in the duct tape I tore off Bonte's mouth and punched the side window of the guard station, shattering it. Just as I had hoped, Congolese building standards even for European countries had not caught up to the Western use of safety glass, so I had some nice big shards to choose from.

I chose the biggest and was through Bonte's bonds in seconds.

"I cannot feel my hands and my feet well, Monsieur Brett."

"Your blood's going to start pumping real good here in about five seconds," I said, and shoved one of the heavy eggs into his arms. "These are all that's between us and that dinosaur. Let's give her what she—"

*WHOMP!* The mass of humanity hit the guardhouse and flooded around it like a river around a monster island. We were stuck. Another *HRRRRRRRANNNNNNNNH* slammed into our eardrums, and it definitely came from *this* side of the river. We had no way to get past the wall of humanity, and she was coming for the eggs and the unlucky humans she would gladly chew into a slurry.

"There's no time to get the eggs on the shore!" I had to yell to Bonte, even though he was standing right to me. "We have to *think*."

Pushed by the waves of miners, Ellie nonetheless was able to switch direction and join us on the lee side of the guard station. "There's no time to get the eggs on the shore!" she said, making Bonte and me laugh stupidly. She gave us a quizzical look but then shot a quick glance at the Vermeulen bunker and tore the walkie-talkie off Bonte's head.

"*Merde!*"

"*Pardon!*" she said, but focused on mashing the talk button. "Atari! Mister Bushnell! We give up! We're coming in!"

His laugh came through the bit of static at this greater range. "I don't know … it was kind of a limited time offer."

"What do you want?" she snapped into the phone. "Sex? Brett's humiliation? You want us to work for you? *Tell me!*"

He laughed even harder and said through his mirth, "I'll take *all* of those! Come to the front door. We can open it since the miners—"

"No, the spinosaurus will be too close!" she said, and we could see Mama sniffing at and stomping at everything she could. She was still far enough away that we would have time to run around the building, especially if we left the eggs right here to let Mama discover.

"I'm sorry, the *what?*" Atari said, obviously in no hurry. "I don't know about any spinosaurus."

"Fine—the *Kasai Rex*, the *Kasai Rex!*" she screamed with approaching panic into the radio.

"Ha! Very good. All right, yes, come to the back. Someone will have the door open for your dumb asses."

The insults didn't matter; all that mattered was running in a beeline around the side of the building and to the back as fast as we could. The spinosaur would see us exposed for maybe ten seconds as we made the dash, but that might not be enough for her to comprehend what was happening. She would smell the eggs, though, and then the jog would be up.

"Count of three," I said. "One, two, *go!*"

Bonte popped out first, with Ellie next and me in the rear. But our driver didn't make it two steps before his still-numb feet betrayed him, and he tripped forward.

Onto the egg.

Breaking the egg.

Covering him with the albumen and sticky fluid that surrounded what was an almost-ready-to-hatch baby spinosaur.

Mama whipped her head to the side and saw, *smelled*, what had happened, and released a sound of fury so deep that it came out as a garbled choking, extremely loud *squeak* as she turned to come at us.

Bonte shouted, "You go! *You go!*" and got up on his feet and ran in *front* of the bunker building, distracting her from Ellie and me and bringing it all to bear on poor Bonte.

Without another sound, Ellie grabbed one of the eggs and we ran with them toward the side of the building. We saw that Bonte had thrown himself against the bolted front door, smearing the egg's fluid all over it and the walls as the enraged dinosaur ran to destroy him. His final act of defiance would be to smear the baby dinosaur egg fluids all over the Vermeulen door.

*Why would he do that? Why the door?* I wondered frantically as we high-tailed it around the building and saw that, true to his word for once, Atari had one of his lackeys, Melanie I believe, draw *in* a secret door with no knob or any discerning features on it to differentiate it from the building's wall on either side. I would have walked right by it, never mind seeing it while running.

We started hitting the brakes as we got near the door Melanie was holding open, and Ellie asked, "Brett—what do we do with the eggs?"

Melanie just shrugged. She didn't seem to care or even be terribly curious about our carrying these massive ovoids.

Then it hit me what Bonte did, the purpose of his final action against the company that would kill his family—he spread the egg innards all over the weakest spot in the building, even if it was bolted shut: the door. Mama Spinosaurus would associate the door—maybe the building as a whole—as the killer of her baby, and attack at that spot. Anywhere she smelled her destroyed offspring, she would attack. He would die, but his death would punish the killers of so many of his friends and those who would take his family from him.

"Take your egg inside," I whispered to Ellie, although Melanie was more concerned with not being at the door when the monster was loose. So I said to the cowardly Vermeulen employee, "Miss, I'll close the door—you get to safety."

She darted inside and I set the egg I carried right in the doorjamb—and slammed the door, bursting the egg and also keeping the door from shutting since the almost-fully formed baby Spinosaur lay across the opening. Everyone inside had run to their safe places, leaving the former safe place for the miners—that tremendous empty space where the poor bastards slept in on sleeping bags—completely wasted.

Ellie had waited for me and we got to the middle of the building, then squatted down next to a support pillar in the large empty space. The dinosaur outside was smashing against the front door with a ferocity that shook the entire building, but her bulk against the small size and reinforcements against the door wouldn't allow her enough leverage to make any progress on getting inside.

Then the shaking stopped and Mama let out another shrieking roar. I tried hard not to think about the rarity and preciousness of the eggs I was breaking so flippantly, the killing. But I rationalized that she had more eggs that would now not be stolen, self-serving as that may have been. I had a plan, and now that I could hear her coming around the other end of the building where the fresher egg—and partially open door—awaited, I gave Ellie the choice of staying where she was or coming with me. "Neither way is safe," I said, "because nothing is safe."

She held the egg gently and looked at it for a moment before asking me, "Where are we going?"

"To Mister Bushnell's new office. We have something to share with him, don't we?"

Ellie again looked at the egg, ruefully this time. "Yes, we do," she said, and took my hand to get herself up. We quickly reached Vermeulen's former and Atari's current vault-like office on the other side of the building, and I banged hard on the door *just* as the spinosaur found the next broken egg and screamed.

"*What?*" came the annoyed yell from inside.

"It's me and Ellie, come to make good on our promises!" I yelled. "Sex, humiliation—all your greatest dreams come true!"

I heard him laugh and seconds later we could hear a code being punched in and sliding locks being retracted on the office door. At the exact second that knob started to turn, Mama must have realized she could get her two-foot-long claws into the outside doorjamb and *rip* the entire door off its hidden hinges. She was coming in that door, and our only chance at survival was getting through this one.

The noise was unreal as she stuck her snout against the door, the jellied insides of her babies coating the very tip, and *ROARED*. I could hear the employees screaming in abject terror—something they probably found amusing when the miners were doing it when locked outside at the bolted front door.

The office door knob stopped turning as soon as the roar started, but it was too late for Atari to change his mind—I got my hand on it and continued its twist, throwing my shoulder against the door and blasting it open, knocking the fat black kid to the floor. I followed his eyes to the .357 Magnum still on his desk, and we both lunged for it. I got there first, and he curled into a ball in a pathetic attempt to protect himself.

But I didn't want the gun so I could shoot *him.*

I cocked the Magnum and shot six smoking holes into his door. A smaller-caliber handgun might not have penetrated that steel, but the .357 did.

When he counted all six bullets fired, Atari untucked his head and said, "What the hell'd you do *that* for?"

"Ventilation," I said, and nodded to Ellie, who raised the last egg up and brought it down forcefully onto Atari's evil, rotten head. The egg was pierced by his skull and he ended up wearing the egg like a full-face mask as the albumen and bloody yolk poured out, soaking him and his new suit in a scent Mama would find irresistible. The fetus flopped out, wiggling a little bit but not quite developed enough to survive yet.

He got the now-empty shell off his head and screamed at us: "You assholes are *crazy*! You think I'm not gonna kill you for this? *Both* of you?"

A dozen voices cried out and kept screaming as Mama pushed her head through the back door and roared again at the little pieces of food running around inside. The look on Atari's face was almost indescribable, but if I had to say, I'd call it *THIS IS NOT HAPPENING* followed by *I JUST SHIT MY PANTS.*

"Shut the door! Lock it! We're safe in here!" Atari pleaded, as if he hadn't just promised to kill us for drowning his suit in egg and aborted spinosaur fetus.

I smiled and said, "You'll never be safe again, asshole" and, before he could scramble to his feet, I took the butt of the .357 and brought it down on his knee so hard I thought I bent the metal. Atari pierced the air with his screams and remained on the floor, his broken kneecap not allowing him to stand, let alone cross the room to shut and bolt the door. "No, please—I can get you *millions* right now! Just shut the door! *Please!*"

"Your girlfriend will be right in, *sir*," Ellie said, and we made motions like we were sweeping the egg's scent through the new ventilation holes I had provided. "She'll love your new cologne."

Atari hadn't stopped screaming from the kneecapping, but now that he knew what was about to happen, his pitch rose even higher and the promises he made even grander. We laughed at them and ran, leaving the door open for good measure.

The spinosaur lifted a large part of the back wall of the building now and it broke to pieces that rained off the sides of her snout. Vermeulen's staff of rotten shits had all ensconced themselves somewhere, and maybe they'd be safe. Depended on how much of the building Mama decided to destroy in the flames of her anger.

Ellie and I flat-out *ran* to the front door. I struggled to get the reinforcements down out of their cradles while Ellie started unbolting everything as fast as she could. But then the building shook like an earthquake was bringing it down.

It was the spinosaur rearing up on her hind legs to rip half of the bunker's roof off. Much of it crashed back inside, but that didn't matter—Mama was *in* now ... and heading straight for Vermeulen's vault.

We had to get *out*, out of the building before it all came down in top of us, but for the immediate moment we were mesmerized as the dinosaur got the open door of the office and screamed louder than ten jet engines, so hard that papers from the office swept out the open door and spinosaur bile was shot inside like bullets. If Atari wasn't dead, both of his eardrums were burst, pain no one who hasn't experienced it can even imagine.

Then she shoved what she could of her snout inside and—Atari wasn't dead, we could hear his pleading screams—dragged the treacherous bastard out by his legs. My knees almost buckled even trying to think about what *that* would feel like after a kneecapping.

Sorry, but I enjoyed every second of it.

She flipped the heavy man like a salmon in the mouth of a bear and clamped him in her jaws—but didn't crunch him to pieces. He was still alive, we knew that from watching him struggle and hearing him shriek, but she didn't chew. She carried him, keeping an inescapable hold on him in the jaws, but then backed up, her tail whipping against the part of the bunker I assumed the office workers were in. It crumbled, and I couldn't tell if I heard any fresh screams because the walls collapsing was tremendously loud.

Seeing those walls go was like a whipcrack getting Ellie and me back to work at unlocking the front door before this part collapsed as well. Finally, we got it open and all at once we spilled outside in the purple sky of the approaching dawn. The flattened tent city was visible in the early morning light, but no bodies were in them this time, no fires, no bloody horror.

There was one human form, however, not too far from the door, and although it was pretty much face-down, it pulled itself along by its arms and elbows.

"Bonte?" Ellie said, and hurried to him, lifting his face out of the clay.

He looked terrible, eyes blackened and face puffy from abuse, but he smiled at us with no more missing teeth than before. "Miss Ellie! Monsieur Brett! May the ancestors be praised!" he said with joy, and added without changing his tone, "My legs are also broken!"

Ellie started to say something soothing, but we were interrupted by the spectacle of the ninety-foot-long impossible dinosaur coming around what was left of the front of the building, pausing to look our way and stare at us before she turned away and slid her enormity into the deep waters of the river. In a few seconds, she came up onto the other side and disappeared into the tunnel in the foliage on the opposite shore.

"Did you see that?" Ellie asked. "She was still carrying Atari in her jaws."

"I saw … and heard, too." I'd be hearing those screams in my nightmares for a long time to come, I bet.

"Bonte, what happened? *How are you alive?*"

He chuckled a little at that, even though it obviously made the pain flare up. "She bashed at the door and bashed and bashed. Then she picked me up with her mouth, breaking my poor legs as she held on to me." He blinked, obviously amazed by his own story. "Then she sniffed the air real good and dropped me onto the ground. Right on my legs, *sacre bleu …*"

Ellie looked at me. "Why would she pick him up, and then Atari? Why didn't she just rip them apart like the others?"

"You're the cryptid expert."

"I bet your son could have told us," she said sweetly. She was right: sharing my memories with her did help keep him alive. "Any theories, Daddy-O?"

It only took me a moment to connect the nearly complete spinosaur babies inside the eggs with what Mama did first with Bonte, and then, when she smelled even more of her young around the building, dropped him and got Atari in her jaws. "The remaining babies are ready to hatch," I said. "They're gonna be hungry."

"Holy shit," Ellie said, her eyes wide and a hand held to her mouth, and then she laughed really hard. "That's horrible!"

I laughed too, and Bonte even managed another smile. I knelt and leaned down to him and said, "Where's the car?"

"Right outside the gate."

"How far is the hospital?"

"Everything is close in Tshikapa. You can't miss it," he said, and passed out.

I got him up onto my shoulders in the fireman carry—if he hadn't lost consciousness from the pain a minute earlier, he would have now. I could feel the broken pieces inside his legs. But he was alive and not ripped to pieces by baby dinosaurs like Atari would be very soon, so all things considered I think we could call it a win.

# EPILOGUE

I sat in the tent with Ellie, helping her mourn Gregory and also the fact that she got no footage of her first real cryptid.

"Yeah, but you know where they are now," I said, giving her a little kiss. "You can come back and do a real documentary, not this *Cryptids Alive!* malarkey."

"*Malarkey?*" she repeated with a smirk. "What are you, Sam Spade?"

"Hogwash? Foofaraw? Mishegoss?"

"You can stick to 'bullshit,' you bad man." Her smile was real and beautiful. It fell, though, as she saw me look over at the satellite phone through the flap to the bedroom I had used it in when I talked to … whoever I talked to. "Are you going to call them?"

"I'm gonna give it a shot," I said weakly. "The Vermeulen building is rubble—if my new identity paperwork was in there, it's gone now. I have no idea what will happen when I dial that number, which way it will go. I'll know within five seconds whether my life is over."

"Then the call can wait. Come here," Ellie said, and pulled me to her. We shuffled to the sleeping bag inside her room in the tent. "If your life might be over, then why not spend the rest of it with me?"

## CHECK OUT OTHER GREAT DINOSAUR THRILLERS

# THE VALLEY
## by Rick Jones

In a dystopian future, a self-contained valley in Argentina serves as the 'far arena' for those convicted of a crime. Inside the Valley: carnivorous dinosaurs generated from preserved DNA. The goal: cross the Valley to get to the Gates of Freedom. The chance of survival: no one has ever completed the journey. Convicted of crimes with little or no merit, Ben Peyton and others must battle their way across fields filled with the world's deadliest apex predators in order to reach salvation. All the while the journey is caught on cameras and broadcast to the world as a reality show, the deaths and killings real, the macabre appetite of the audience needing to be satiated as Ben Peyton leads his team to escape not only from a legal system that's more interested in entertainment than in justice, but also from the predators of the Valley.

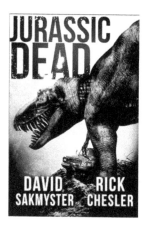

# JURASSIC DEAD
## by Rick Chesler & David Sakmyster

An Antarctic research team hoping to study microbial organisms in an underground lake discovers something far more amazing: perfectly preserved dinosaur corpses. After one thaws and wakes ravenously hungry, it becomes apparent that death, like life, will find a way.

Environmental activist Alex Ramirez, son of the expedition's paleontologist, came to Antarctica to defend the organisms from extinction, but soon learns that it is the human race that needs protecting.

# CHECK OUT OTHER GREAT DINOSAUR THRILLERS

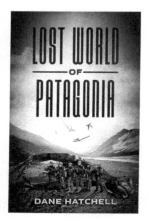

## LOST WORLD OF PATAGONIA
by Dane Hatchell

An earthquake opens a path to a land hidden for millions of years. Under the guise of finding cryptid animals, Ace Corporation sends Alex Klasse, a Cryptozoologist and university professor, his associates, and a band of mercenaries to explore the Lost World of Patagonia. The crew boards a nuclear powered All-Terrain Tracked Carrier and takes a harrowing ride into the unknown.

The expedition soon discovers prehistoric creatures still exist. But the dangers won't prevent a sub-team from leaving the group in search of rare jewels. Tensions run high as personalities clash, and man proves to be just as deadly as the dinosaurs that roam the countryside.

Lost World of Patagonia is a prehistoric thriller filled with murder, mayhem, and savage dinosaur action.

## SAVAGE ISLAND
by Alan Spencer

Somewhere in the Atlantic Ocean, an uncharted island has been used for the illegal dumping of chemicals and pollutants for years by Globo Corp's. Private investigator Pierce Range will learn plenty about the evil conglomerate when Susan Branch, an environmentalist from The Green Project, hires him to join the expedition to save her kidnapped father from Globo Corp's evil hands.

Things go to hell in a hurry once the team reaches the island. The bloodthirsty dinosaurs and voracious cannibals are only the beginning of the fight for survival. Pierce must unlock the mysteries surrounding the toxic operation and somehow remain in one piece to complete the rescue mission.

Ratchet up the body count, because this mission will leave the killing floor soaked in blood and chewed up corpses. When the insane battle ends, will there by anybody left alive to survive Savage Island?

CPSIA information can be obtained
at www.ICGtesting.com
Printed in the USA
LVHW031940220122
709005LV00008B/1291